THE SCAVENGER

SURVIVAL OF THE FITTEST

THE SCAVENGER

By

C.t. Lowry

Creedom Publishing Company
Philadelphia, Pennsylvania

The Cataloging-in-Publication Data is on file at the Library of Congress.

Creedom Publishing Company

Visit the website at:
www.CreedomPublishing.com

Cover Design: Wilde Designs

ISBN-13: 978-1-946897-82-4
ISBN-10: 1-946897-82-5
LCCN: 2017913311

Printed in the United States of America
11 10 9 8 7 6 5 4 3 2

For,

HUMANITY

CHAPTER

1

HOLDING HIS BABY GIRL'S lifeless body was one of the worst feelings Kyle had to endure in his life. He couldn't help but reminisce on the first day he laid eyes on her in the Labor and Delivery room at Penn Hospital. She was the spitting image of him. Now, it was fourteen years later and she was no longer with him. Tears poured from his bloodshot eyes and pain masked his face. Pulling her tight into his body, he buried his nose into the top of her head, engulfing in the aroma of her shampoo. He immediately recognized the strawberry scent of the Herbal Essence shampoo Chloe would always beg him to pick up from the market. It all had to be a bad nightmare; this couldn't be a reality. No parent should ever have to outlive his or her child. "It's all over now princess, you don't have to suffer anymore," he whispered before puckering his dry lips and kissing her on the forehead. "I love you."

It was humid and muggy. The summer heat was blaring through the small attic window. Kyle looked over at his wife, Jacqui, who was still in shock. Her soul looked as if it was ripped from her body and thrown into the pits of Hell. "Why? Why did it have to be her? She was so young and so innocent," Jacqui murmured.

Unable to console his wife, Kyle pulled his daughter in close again. Her thin body was wrapped in his stocky arms. After brushing her hair away from her face, he leaned in and kissed her forehead once more. He had no answer for his wife and no remedy for their pain. What could he possibly say to her? In the back of his mind, he knew she was partially responsible for his daughter's death. How could he comfort someone he felt so much anger towards? Keeping space between them would be best for them both. If she knew how he truly felt, she would be devastated.

"We should have left when we had the chance," Kyle said while avoiding making direct eye contact with Jacqui.

"Don't say that."

"I'm serious; we should have just —"

Jacqui cut him off, "I said don't fucking say it. We didn't know those monsters were coming here."

The consistent tears magnified Jacqui's gray eyes. They were like two chrome faucets that someone had turned on, as tears pooled in her eyes. There was nothing but fear and grief running through Jacqui's body. She crept up to the window and scanned the exterior of their house. The scan was brief, once her teary eyes locked on the two dead bodies that were left to rot in front their home. Jacqui knew her husband's military experience would come in handy one day, but she never fathomed the idea of witnessing him take a life. The barrel of the rifle was still smoking as it was propped up against the window.

"Kyle, do you think more of them will come?"

"I know more will come," he replied sternly. "I just need to know that you will be ready when they do."

"You know this is hard for me. Everything is so different now and we lost so many people —"

"— and we will lose more. Especially if we aren't prepared. We must prepare for the worst."

"That's easy for you to say. You were a fuckin' Marine for God's sake. I was just a school teacher. I never shot a gun and I damn sure never killed anyone."

"You just killed our fuckin' daughter," Kyle barked. A mixture of saliva and tears spewed from his mouth with every word he spoke. His pain quickly turned into rage and it was all aimed towards his wife.

"Really Kyle? Are you fuckin' serious?" Jacqui was heartbroken and dropped to her knees. "I didn't mean for it to happen," she mumbled through her sobs.

"All you had to do was put your mask on and you couldn't even do that. I told you not to take it off before those two assholes threw in those gas canisters and the first thing you did was put it down."

"I didn't ask Chloe to give me her mask. I told her not to and she did anyway. Now my baby is gone." The sobbing increased greatly as Jacqui came to grips with the fact that her negligence caused her daughter's death.

Seeing his wife in such turmoil calmed Kyle down a tad bit. He laid Chloe's lifeless body on the bedroom floor and embraced Jacqui. Her tears soaked through his torn t-shirt. Swallowing back the emotional bulge in his throat, Kyle looked away from Chloe's body; tears flowing from his eyes. Although it was the perfect time to console Jacqui, there was still an urgency to stay alive. The danger was still lurking.

Kyle did his best to seal the gaps around the bedroom door and the air vents, to prevent the deadly gas from seeping through to the room they were held up in. He picked up the skills during the time he served in Iraq. Kyle usually made due with a cot and a blanket in his outdoor camp in Baghdad. When it was time for him to spend nights in small shacks, it was his responsibility to seal the doors to prevent sand and dust from entering the clear air he had indoors, so sealing a small bedroom was nothing to him. If the gas reached them, they would face the same fate as their daughter and half of the country. A chemical gas that was created by the U.S. Government for the purposes of fighting the war on terror had wiped out fifty percent of the United States population. Not only did the chemical gas kill many people, but it also worked its way onto the black market and was now in the hands of criminals and thugs like the two men Kyle shot dead in front of their house.

"I knew this day would come. I told you this all would happen," he muttered. "Everyone thought I was crazy for stocking up on MRE's, can goods, and ammo. Oh and not to mention these gas masks," he stated while gripping the mask that was dangling from his neck.

Kyle literally prepared for the worst and that is exactly what occurred several months prior. Protests had become a common occurrence all across the country. They went from peaceful, to combative and finally reached the level of full out violence. Citizens were attacking police officers during the protests and line of duty deaths nearly quadrupled across the country. America never experienced incidents of such magnitude before. The military had to be brought in to assist local police departments. At that point, the police stopped policing and that is when it all went downhill. Martial law, criminals running wild, and the massive attack on the white house. It was complete chaos across the country. To make matters worse, the military put out a warning for everyone to stay indoors and that is when the chemical attacks began taking place. The very weapons that were created to fight against the enemies overseas were now being used on American citizens. The intention of the gas attacks was to eliminate all threats, which were said to be anyone violating Martial Law. Therefore, if you were on the streets after ten o'clock at night, you were considered a threat to the government. Those weaponized chemicals wiped out almost half of the United States population, including children. Some families looked at it as the government overreacting, so they did not follow the specific orders that were given out regarding sealing up their homes.

Millions died in their sleep, unaware the gas had worked its way inside their homes. There had been rumors of some casualties mutating as an irreversible effect of some of the experimental gas the military used, but no one knew for sure.

CHAPTER

2

The sound of loud engines and blaring heavy metal music could be heard coming from outside. Kyle crouched down and peeked out the cracked glass in the window. He saw two black Ford F-350 pickup trucks driving up the street, along with a large U-Haul truck. His nerves were jumping through his body, as he glanced over at the silver Ford F-150 that was parked in the middle of the street. The occupants of that truck were in front of his home, with their brains splattered all over the sidewalk. A result of two perfectly placed headshots. Kyle had a feeling that the gang pulling up was associated with the two miscreants that tried breaking into his home. This would not end well once they spotted the bodies. They would surely want revenge, so he had to be ready for them. He dropped the magazine from his rifle to check his remaining ammo. He had about ten rounds left in the thirty-round magazine and that was not going to be enough. There was plenty of spare ammo in the basement, but Kyle did not want to risk opening the door and possibly letting the lethal gas seep in the room. Ten rounds were more than enough ammo to take on a few more scoundrels, but if they were armed, he would need a lot more ammo to be effective in a gun battle.

As Kyle suspected, they pulled up directly behind the silver F-150. Based on the urgency in which they exited their vehicles, it was obvious to Kyle they spotted the bodies of their associates. There were eight of them total and they had their guns pointed in every direction. Their movements were fluid as if they trained regularly, but did not appear to be military. Kyle sized up each miscreant and the weapon they possessed. They were all toting handguns, except a tall woman who was handling an AR-15. She seemed very familiar with the weapon based on her posture.

"Find out who the fuck did this," the mysterious woman ordered.

Her fierce grimace and commanding voice had the group scattering like roaches.

"What's going on?" Jacqui asked once she noticed Kyle lingering at the window.

"Shhhh," he replied. He slowly grabbed his rifle and aimed it towards the woman, who was now standing in the bed of the silver F-150. The sun rays soaked into her dark skin, which was visible because she was only wearing an off-white tank top that was riddled with blood splatter. She was probably around five foot nine inches but looked taller than six feet if you took into account her large afro. The mirrored Ray Ban sunglasses she sported sat perfectly on her round face.

Although one of the lenses appeared to be cracked, she still rocked them as if they were fresh out the store.

"Search every single home and kill anyone inside. Start with this house," she barked as she pointed to Kyle and Jacqui's home. It was an obvious choice, seeing as though the rotting bodies rested in front of the three-story row home.

Three men worked their way to the front door and the others started walking towards neighboring houses. Kyle carefully watched as the three approached. One of them had his gun aimed at the bedroom window but never noticed Kyle looking down at them. The cracks in the glass obstructed his view of the shadowy figure lingering in the corner of the window. Kyle's aim drifted towards one of the men and he slowly squeezed the trigger on his Springfield Saint. The shot rang off and another successful headshot was executed. The man fell to the ground and blood began to pool around his head. The other members of the small militia took cover and their eyes were now focused across the street from Kyle's home. His plan actually worked. He shot one of the goons across the street, which made the rest of the gang believe the assault was coming from another home, leaving them vulnerable. Kyle felt a little bad and hoped an innocent family was not inside the home the body dropped in front of because they would surely become the militia's new targets. If there was a family still at the residence, they probably would not survive an attack from the militia. Hopefully, they made it out during the evacuation warnings a few days prior.

Shots began to ring off and Kyle backed out the window. Jacqui ducked down and stayed away from the exposed area of the room. Kyle waited a few seconds, then peeked back out and noticed the gunshot holes that decorated the house across the street. The woman with the broken Ray Bans was nowhere in sight, but the other members of the militia began making their way to the home. Kyle lifted his rifle again and let off two more shots, dropping two more members.

"Get back, get back," one of the men yelled. Each of the miscreants began making their way back to the trucks. Kyle only had seven shots left and had to make them count. He took up aim at one of the F-150s and let off a shot meant for the occupant in the driver's seat. The rear windshield shattered but no one exited the truck.

"Fuck," Kyle yelled, disappointed at the fact he didn't know if his shot attempt was successful. If he had his ammo from the basement, each truck would look like a slice of Swiss cheese. About five minutes went by and there was no movement from the militia.

"What's going on out there?" Jacqui asked, noticing how quiet the outside became.

"I have no idea." A stern look was on Kyle's face as he watched diligently for any type of movement.

Finally, one of the men exited the passenger seat of the U-Haul truck and climbed on top. Kyle had the opportunity to attempt a shot at the male but was too focused on what he was doing on top of the truck. He crawled to the rear of the truck and grabbed a rope that was affixed to the roof. The rope was also attached to the door latch. The woman suddenly appeared from the F-150, but she was not wearing her sunglasses. She had a red, green, and black bandana tied around her face that covered her nose and mouth. She toted a pistol-grip shotgun and blasted the front door of the home, four times. The door was literally ripped off the hinges. After blasting the door, she threw a gas canister into the home. The canister contained the chemical gas that stole the lives of millions of citizens, including Chloe. The same gas was finally dispersing from the lower level of the couple's home, but he still ensured it did not make its way into the bedroom. Kyle recognized the canister as being similar to the one the initial miscreants tossed in his home. Once the woman reentered the F-150, the man on top of the U-Haul pulled the rope, which opened the rear door. Kyle looked to see what was inside the truck. He figured they had more personnel to carry out their heinous assaults on the innocent. However, what he witnessed was much worse as his mouth dropped to the floor.

Some type of creature crawled out the rear of the U-Haul truck and was nothing like any animal he had ever seen. Once it was set free, the trucks pulled off. The creature lingered in the street for a while. It was very hairy with large claws. It had mannerisms similar to a gorilla, using its knuckles for stability as it roamed the unfamiliar territory. Kyle could not get a good look at its facial features, but its shoulders and back were extremely broad. The creature began sniffing the ground as it brushed past parked vehicles. Its strength was unreal and Kyle watched it climb on the hood of the car and crush it. This made Jacqui extremely nervous, as she peeked out the window and saw a beast that possessed so much strength. The beast caught the scent from the chemical gas currently dispensing from the canister. The orange gas was escaping from the broken window and doorway that occurred when the militia began its assault on the home. Suddenly the hideous creature took off running into the home.

"What the hell was that?" Jacqui asked as she backed out the window.

"I have no fucking clue. I really don't know what the hell that was."

"Where did it come from?"

"The back of that U-Haul truck."

"How the hell did they get it in that U-Haul?"

"I don't know, but whatever it is we better hope we don't have to deal with it."

"Kyle I'm scared. We should have gotten out of here when we had the chance. When they sent out those evacuation warnings."

"Where would we have gone? This shit is a national epidemic, not local. National."

"I don't know where we would have gone, but we wouldn't be prisoners in our own damn home."

"Yeah, you would probably be dead."

Jacqui felt the sarcasm in Kyle's last remark and crawled over to Chloe's body. When she heard Kyle say *dead*, she sat back and thought of all the warnings he gave her.

CHAPTER

3

KYLE COULDN'T HELP BUT stare at Chloe as she brushed back her sandy brown hair from in front of her face. His baby girl was growing up too fast. Although she was just about to enter into ninth grade, her face was buried in catalogs from colleges in the area. She was already picking out the colleges she was interested in attending, with Penn State and Temple Universities leading the pack. With all the time she spent away from her dad while he was overseas, there was no way she was going far from home.

"Dad, Texas or Texas Tech?" she asked jokingly.

Kyle dropped his spoon, causing soggy Honey Nut Cheerios to hit the floor. His face frowned up as his brain registered the question he was asked. "How about CCP?"

"Community College? Dad, I want to get my Bachelor's Degree and it would be too much of a hassle to figure out which classes are transferable. What's wrong with Texas?"

"I didn't say anything was wrong with Texas. It's just that you could save your mom and me a lot of money if you went to CCP and you would be here with us. That would give us enough time to convince you to attend Drexel or LaSalle." Kyle had a huge grin on his face, laying out his plan to keep his baby girl local.

Chloe laughed because she knew her father was serious about her staying close to home. He refused to accept the possibility of his baby girl moving hundreds of miles away. Although Chloe was four years from the big decision, the fact she was so dedicated to her goal was fascinating to her parents.

"Come on Chloe, you know your father gets all worked up when you start talking about college," Jacqui said as she sat a plate of pancakes in the center of the dining room table.

"But mom, those top universities in states like Texas and Florida have great athletic programs too. Imagine all the amazing football games dad can come watch. You know he loves football."

"First of all, Philadelphia has great sports teams. We don't need to go all the way down to Texas when we can just turn on the television if we really want to see some Longhorn football."

The aroma of sizzling bacon made its way to Kyle's nose. He pushed the cereal bowl aside, making room for breakfast that would be fit for a king. Jacqui placed the platter in front of Kyle that consisted of scrambled eggs topped with shredded cheddar cheese, thick cut bacon, sage turkey sausage, seasoned home fries, and warm biscuits that were fresh out the oven. "See Chloe, you'll be missing all this," he muttered while stabbing his sausage with a fork and stuffing his face.

Kyle could not ask for anything more in life; he was truly a blessed man. He watched as Chloe stood and reached into one of the cabinets. She looked at her father, smiled, and pulled out a plastic shopping bag. Placing the bag on the countertop, Chloe left it exposed so Kyle could look inside and see the contents. He smirked when he observed the canned goods that filled the bag. She was pleased to see his joyful response. "Mom let me get them when we were at the market yesterday."

"That's right," Jacqui agreed. "It seems like you have a little helper for the zombie apocalypse you're planning for."

Kyle could not help but laugh at her statement, knowing he wanted to tear the bag open and stock each can fit neatly in the basement, alongside the many others that filled a large shelf. He was a survivalist and Chloe was always curious about how the world would eventually end. He never imagined it would have come so soon and been this devastating.

CHAPTER 4

It was quiet and there was no movement coming from across the street. Kyle was perched up in the window, scanning for the thugs but they never returned. Jacqui was in the corner of the room, continuously rocking Chloe's body as if a miracle was going to occur and she would wake from her eternal slumber. He wanted to tell her to leave the body alone, but he also wanted to give her space to grieve. Jacqui was softly singing Chloe's favorite song, hoping the fine tune would find its way up to heaven and give her baby girl a second chance at life.

CRASH!

The roaring sound forced, Kyle to focus his attention on the house across the street. Initially, things were still but his eyes widened in fear. A beast emerged from the dark, vacant home and worked its way to the middle of the street. Similar to a trained police canine, the beast appeared to be following a scent. It used its moist snout to sniff the ground, parked cars, and even the foggy air. The beast maneuvered through the street as if it was looking for something in particular. Working its way a few feet in every direction, its final resting point was directly in front of Kyle's home. He watched as the beast sniffed the thick, orange fog that slowly disseminated through the creases of the front door and the broken window. The same poisonous fog that suffocated his daughter, and took her innocent life. *It does not affect that thing*, he thought. A part of Kyle was hoping the beast would breathe in the poison and drop dead, but the creature was alive and well.

Kyle raised his rifle and aimed at the beast. He knew missing the shot could cost him his life because it would surely revert to its animal instincts and attack him. The red dot of the AimPoint scope danced around the beast's chest and Kyle's trigger finger began to reach. *I don't even know if this will put it down.* Second-guessing his choice to aim center mass, hoping to send a rifle round directly through its heart, Kyle refocused his aim to the beast's head. *Nothing can survive a headshot*, he thought as he began to take out the slack of the trigger.

HOWL. HOWL.

The loud echoing noise the beast made mimicked that of a wolf. It continued howling, which briefly took Kyle's attention off the shot he was preparing to take and made him focus on the beast's subtle movements. He did not even realize he had subconsciously removed his finger from the trigger of the AR-15. Kyle was more focused on getting to know his target; he had quickly transitioned from a shooter to an observer. Different thoughts ran through his mind, as he wondered why the beast never entered his home. *Something brought this damn thing to the front of my house.*

"Kyyyyyyyle," Jacqui screamed to the top of her lungs. The blood-wrenching scream took his attention completely off the beast outside his home, only for him to look over at Jacqui who was being pinned down by another one. Kyle wasted no time sending two shots through the temple of the beast, freeing Jacqui from its killer grip. This creature was slightly smaller in stature than the one outside and not as hairy. With his rifle still raised, Kyle approached the beast that was sprawled out next to his wife. "Jacqui get up and come here," Kyle ordered, wanting to get her as far away from the beast as possible. He spoke softly, knowing another threat was waiting right outside. "Jacqui, come here," he repeated. It did not take long to realize something was not right. His wife was not responding and blood was visible on her shirt. Kyle dropped his rifle when he saw that a chunk of Jacqui's neck had been ripped away and blood was profusely pouring from the wound. "No baby no. Jacqui get up baby. Come on, don't do this," Kyle pleaded while shaking Jacqui's lifeless body and praying she would embrace him. Still, there was no response. Jacqui was gone.

Kyle rested her body on the floor and covered her body with a small blanket. He could not bear to see the corpse of his wife. He ran over to the window to get eyes on the beast in front of the house. The thick orange fog was spreading, but there was no sign of the beast. It was not anywhere to be found and Kyle saw red. His jaw was clenched and hands balled up into fists, as he stomped towards the bodies. "You motherfucker," Kyle yelled while turning the beast over on its back and placing its hunting knife to its throat. "I'm going to gut you like a fuckin' fish," he stated emotionally. Blood was oozing out the head wounds Kyle inflicted, but he did not care. He decided to behead the dead beast as a form of revenge. This beast was different from the other. Its features more human like than anything else. Teeth were extremely sharp and only its head was covered with hair, rather than its entire body like the other beast. Kyle raised his knife and targeted the mandibular notch for his first strike with the sharp, serrated blade.

"What the fuck," he muttered after seeing more than blood splatter on the neck of the beast. A small white gold necklace rested on the rough skin of the beast's neck. A small charm dangled from the necklace. It was the letter C with small diamonds on the surface of the charm. An exact match to the necklace Kyle bought Chloe on her birthday. His eyes scanned the room, looking for her body. He knew the unthinkable had happened, but he was hoping his eyes would tell him otherwise. There was only one human corpse in the room and it was Jacqui's. Shards of the clothing Chloe wore were on the ground and the remaining pieces were draped over the beast Kyle had put down. *Chloe? Is that my baby?* He carefully examined the beast, which still maintained many of its human features.

Although she was not herself, Kyle could not help but to dwell on the fact he put two bullets in the side of his daughter's head. He also felt that he wasn't there to protect his wife. He wondered what happened to Chloe and what transformed her. Pools of tears filled his eyes as he hunkered down in the corner and released his emotions. For a man whose family never saw him cry, his heart was in shambles. Kyle always kept things bottled up, but on this day, his emotions got the best of him.

CHAPTER 5

KYLE WORKED HIS WAY down the street. He was a broken man. If losing his daughter wasn't enough, the loss of his wife sent him over the edge. He scaled each building with his rifle pointed at every window and door he passed. An orange fog filled the streets and made it very difficult to see, especially while wearing his gas mask. It was the remanence of the chemical warfare that took place and centuries of pollution. Breathing in the polluted air would be a fatal mistake.

Kyle was about two miles from his home and there was no sign of life. The streets were cluttered with abandoned cars and mauled bodies, adults, and children. Unfortunately, the gruesome sights took Kyle back to the days he was deployed overseas. He would see similar sights, as they trenched through locations where suicide bombers and other types of terrorists had attacked. There were piles of victims that filled the roads. Occasionally peeking in unoccupied vehicles, he searched for weapons, food, or any valuables that would be useful on his journey through the unknown. Each search resulted in no substantial findings. He would only recover a few sweatshirts and hats that would come in handy to fuel a fire or a wardrobe change.

Kyle continued on what seemed like a never-ending journey. He was now approaching the five-mile marker and needed a quick break. He was in good shape and would usually run close to five miles every other day for exercise, but he had to get the mask off and hydrate himself. Getting into a home would be ideal seeing as though he would be able to rest and develop some type of plan. As he continued scaling homes, he turned doorknobs searching for any home that was unlocked. Several homes had been broken into, which made them useless because the gas had already seeped in. Walking into one of them would be like jumping in a casket and closing the lid.

He checked approximately twenty homes before turning a knob that opened up into a three-bedroom row home. With his rifle up, Kyle flowed through the residence. The last thing he needed was another confrontation. Although he would be able to hold off a small army with all the ammunition he loaded up in his duffel bag before the journey. He raided his basement and brought along the gas masks that once belonged to his family. Starting on the first floor, he checked the living room and worked his way to the kitchen.

"Frag out."

BOOM!

The loud explosion was followed up by shuffling feet and gunshots as the troops made contact with an insurgent. They turned the corner of the room and the bearded man began shooting from the behind an island in the kitchen. Rounds filled his chest as the troops returned fire, without hesitation.

"Agh, I'm hit," one of the troops yelled, grimacing in pain.

"Soldier, where are you hit?"

"In the leg, sir," he replied as he was hoisted onto a dusty table. Blood was squirting from the leg wound, which meant the possibility of a severed artery. With the bulky gear he was wearing, the injured troop could not see the severity of his injury. The soaked uniform pants clung to his leg, revealing how much blood he was losing. The other troops continued clearing the small home, but two stayed behind with the injured.

"Ok, just put some pressure on it and I will apply the tourniquet."

"Captain Quinn."

"Yes, soldier."

"If I don't make it, tell my wife and kid I love them."

"You're going to tell them yourself soldier," Kyle replied as he tightened the tourniquet, stopping the blood from continuing to squirt from the gunshot wound.

Everything was neat and orderly. It seemed very odd that this home was in such a state. After clearing the kitchen, Kyle checked the second floor. The three bedrooms and bathrooms were clear and based on the setup, an elderly couple more than likely resided at the home. Each bedroom was made up, but dust covered the woodwork in two of the three bedrooms. Pictures of the couple and their family were on display throughout the home.

Kyle made his way back downstairs and locked the door. He performed his usual routine, sealing all seams and cracks. The air in the home was clear, which was an obvious sign that the chemical gas had not entered. Kyle removed his mask and took a deep breath.

"Ahhhhh, fresh air," he announced.

He placed his duffel bag and rifle down and peeked out the front window to ensure he wasn't being followed. Kyle repositioned his belt that was securing a nine-millimeter handgun in his waistband, along with a forty caliber Glock in a drop holster.

"Let's see what's in this damn kitchen."

Rummaging through the refrigerator and cabinets, Kyle came out with two cans of peaches, some beef jerky, and a bottle of Jameson Irish Whiskey. He plopped on the living room couch and wasted no time devouring the jerky.

You and that damn liquor Kyle, I swear that's all you care about. Jacqui's voice echoed in his mind as his dry lips kissed the rim of the bottle. At that point, it seemed as if the tears were pouring faster than the whiskey as Kyle's head tilted back to enjoy the strong liquor that coated his throat. He lost his whole world and each minute that went by was a battle to find a reason to stay alive. Besides the images of his wife and daughter, Kyle's memory focused on the sight of the brazen woman standing in the bed of the truck, ready to wreak havoc on innocent lives. Her afro stood tall and souls lifted with each round fired from the weapons her militia toted. He vowed to make her and everyone she cared about suffer, in many ways. That serious vow would be kept.

CHAPTER

6

The odor of fresh coffee stimulated Kyle's senses. He was watching television with Chloe, but couldn't help but follow the scent to find out where it was coming from. Jacqui walked over and handed him a large mug. "Extra sugar and cream," she muttered, knowing it was exactly how her man liked it.

"Thanks, baby," he said. His large palm smacked her rear end when she turned to return to the kitchen.

"That is so disgusting," Chloe said, referring to her parent's odd display of affection.

"It wasn't disgusting when we made you, was it?"

"Ewwww, stop it," she replied, chuckling at her father.

"This just in, we are getting reports that there have been numerous attacks at the Alt-Right protests in Center City. A large group of white men and women were marching downtown with Nazi and Confederate flags being waved in the air. The group was chanting, *yelling racial slurs at people and even destroyed property. Thousands of White Supremacists were combatted by an anti-racist group of protestors. We have lost contact with Michael Simons, our reporter that was on scene and in the mix of it all. From what we gathered from the live video footage, it seems to be an all-out war downtown as both sides are now involved in a violent confrontation with each other. We have to warn you that the images you are viewing may not be appropriate for viewers under the age of eighteen. As you can see, people are being attacked with weapons and the police are just standing there. Police officers are literally watching the assaults take place and now it appears that protesters are yelling at the police. Now they are pushing up against the wall of officers and the officers are pushing back. BANG. BANG. BANG. BANG. Oh no, oh no. Shots have been fired. We don't know if the shots were fired by the police officers or at them. We have lost contact with the camera crew but the last visual we had, showed the crowd pushing officers and then shots were fired. I hope things downtown get resolved and no one is seriously hurt. We will be reporting on the protests throughout the night."*

Kyle hugged Chloe tight, covering her eyes with his arm. Although he always spoke to Chloe about the different type of evil people that existed in the world, as a father it was still his job to protect her from those evils. He did not feel it was necessary to watch the news coverage on the violent protests and she didn't feel the need to argue with his decision.

"What the hell has gotten into people?"

Kyle did not even notice Jacqui was leaning on the wall with her eyes glued to the fifty-inch screen. "I have no idea, but they better keep that crap down there."

"I don't even want to imagine that nonsense coming up this way. It would be like the Purge."

"No, it would be like shooting crabs in a barrel."

"Kyle, stop," Jacqui whispered. She hated when he spoke like that in front of Chloe especially while their baby girl was still wrapped in his arms. Kyle looked up at her and smiled, knowing the statement he made was a hundred percent accurate. He would never let someone attempt to harm his family without facing the repercussions. The mere thought of it made his blood boil. "Oh my god," Jacqui yelled out. Kyle and Chloe popped up to see what was causing her so much distress. They noticed her eyes were glued to the television and when they turned to watch, they were both left speechless. A hundred and thirty-eight people dead, Kyle thought. He did not feel it was necessary to repeat the message that displayed on the television.

"Chloe, go up to your room."

"Why dad?"

"You don't need to see this stuff. It's a little too much for a teenager."

"Dad, it's ok. I'm not a baby. Plus, all of this stuff will be on Facebook later and I'm going to see it anyway."

"We have breaking news coming out of Philadelphia. Violent protests have erupted in the

Center City section of the city. Reports are coming in that there are over a hundred people confirmed dead after several armed men opened fire on civilians and police officers. We are told officers returned fire and a gun battle is now currently taking place. The images from the scene are very graphic and we will not be showing them at this time. The Mayor has issued a State of Emergency for the city of Philadelphia and has contacted the Governor for National Guard assistance. If you are watching this, it will be in your best interest to stay out of the downtown area until things clear up in that area. I repeat anyone not in the downtown area at this moment, stay away from this area. If you are in the downtown area, please shelter in place until emergency services arrive. It is not safe to be outside at this moment, as most of you might already know. Just to recap, there are over a hundred people confirmed dead from a violent gun battle currently taking place in downtown Philadelphia."

"I can't keep watching this," Kyle stated as he turned the television off. Jacqui and Chloe were in tears, as news of chaos was being reported from their hometown. It was one thing hearing about devastating news about killings and natural disasters taking place in other countries, but for that type of anarchy to be occurring only thirty minutes away from their home was scary. It was only a matter of time before it spread throughout the rest of the city. Kyle knew this type of event was inevitable with all the hatred people had inside of them for no reason. People were tired of oppression, privilege, and the lack of action on behalf of the government to fix the country's problems. The silence in the room spoke a thousand words. Kyle knew his family was scared and he planned to keep them safe from any dangers that may come knocking on their door. He walked over to his family and gave them the tightest hug. "I would die before I let anything happen to you two."

CHAPTER 7

Loud screams echoed from outside

KYLE HOPPED UP FROM a deep snooze, he hadn't known he entered. The empty whiskey bottle fell to the ground next to the empty cans of peaches. He stumbled over to the window, knocking over a lamp and picture frames. He was more sleepy than drunk, seeing as though he had a very high tolerance for alcohol that developed during the time he served in the military as a young lad. He peeked out into the darkness of night. The only thing visible would be a couple lying on the pavement in front of two beat up minivans. Kyle wasn't sure if the screams came from the couple, but as he looked around, there was no one else in sight.

"Please don't hurt my girlfriend," the husky male begged. Although the man was kneeling on the ground, Kyle could tell he was easily around six-foot-four and two hundred and fifty pounds. The plaid shirt he was wearing was completely snug around his biceps and shoulders. The woman that was next to him was the complete opposite. She was very petite and kept her head buried in the male's arm. The male looked up towards the vehicles; the bright headlights were clearly blinding him. Holding his hand out to block the light did very little, seeing as though both vehicles were at different angles. Blood was pouring from a large laceration over his right eye. There was no telling what type of injuries his girlfriend had sustained.

The pathetic begging was countered by malevolent laughter, coming from the shadows. A large figure emerged from the darkness behind the male. Blonde-haired and standing at about six feet and five inches, the man looked like he was in his mid to late forties. Blood splatter decorated his scruffy beard. His angry grimace was a clear sign that he had no intentions on letting the couple live to see another day. He was pure evil. The type of evil that stole Kyle's family from him, leaving him with nothing but a black heart filled with anger and pain.

"You think begging will make a difference young man? It's a new world order and it's people like you who will now slave and bow down to kings like me."

"For god's sake, we did nothing to you," the hurt male pleaded.

CRACK

The sound of metal smacking against flesh echoed in the silence of the night. Strike after strike, the villainous man delivered continuous blows to the back of his victim. The heavy chain that was wrapped around his hand caused the begging man to sink in a puddle of blood and tears.

"Damn Leo, he's crying like a big baby." Another figure emerged from between the vans. He looked to also be in his forties, but he had a very short and wiry frame. His disheveled appearance and wild hair told Kyle everything he needed to know about the man.

"Yup, the big baby must want a bottle. So Roy, should I fuck his bitch or blow her brains out all over him?"

"I say you do both and make sure you save some for me."

Leo grabbed the woman by one of her legs and dragged her away from her bloodied boyfriend. He began tugging at her skirt, which had lifted and exposed several scrapes on her legs. "No, don't do this. You don't have to do this," she appealed. Tears poured from her eyes like Niagara Falls. She had a feeling the worst was yet to come. "HELP ME," she began screaming at the top of her lungs, before feeling cold metal knocking across her face. The ringing in her ear and sudden blurred vision were the immediate effects of being struck with a hard object. She looked up and was now staring down the barrel of a Mossberg shotgun. Roy's finger was slithering back and forth on the trigger. The finger had an itch and he was ready to scratch it.

BOOM!

The roar of a shot ringing out startled the battered man on the ground. Blood splattered across his attire and his heart sank into his stomach. "Noooooo," he yelled as he crawled over to his girlfriend's body that was covered in blood.

CHAPTER 8

The **ShOtGUn FeLL tO the** ground as Roy's body dropped next to it. A precise shot to his head had ripped off a large chunk of flesh and sent pieces flying in different directions. The couple on the ground was frantically checking their bodies to see if they had been hit, but it was clear someone was targeting Roy. Leo could not believe what happened to his best friend. He had no idea where the shot came from but quickly ran to take cover inside one of the vans. It wasn't long before he emerged with an assault rifle and began firing in every direction, hoping to hit the unknown shooter. He didn't know exactly where the shot that killed his friend came from, so he decided to spray and pray. The street sounded like a war zone as .556 rounds ripped off siding and shattered windows on several homes.

BOOM! BOOM!

The barrel of the shotgun was smoking as it released two slugs that tore open Leo's chest and left his organs on display. Leo had forgotten about the shotgun that fell next to the couple he threatened to kill. The battered man gathered enough strength to pick up the gun and take the soul of the man who tried to rape his girlfriend. The couple held on to the gun and limped into the shadows, with their backs against the front of the home they were snatched out of by the now deceased thugs. Both of them were in complete shock about what just took place.

"Marcus, what are we going to do? Will there be more of them coming?"

"Probably, we have to get the hell out of here."

"Oh my god, look at your face and your back," she stated as her eyes focused on his soaked shirt and the gushing wound over his eye. She helped him up the stone steps, and he limped into the home. The pain was becoming unbearable and nothing they had in their medicine cabinet was going to alleviate his current problem. Resting on the couch seemed to be a good idea. He was weak and tired, and there wasn't much he could physically do. His girlfriend returned from upstairs with a few items they had in the house for an injury, which unfortunately wasn't much. She noticed her boyfriend's eyes were rolling in the back of his head. The last thing she wanted was him falling asleep, especially with a severe head injury. "Marcus. Marcus get up," she yelled as she shook his body in an effort to startle him. She tried for a few more minutes, but her attempts unsuccessful.

"Just leave him be," said a strong voice coming from the front door.

Her soul jumped out her body when she turned and saw a man stepping into the home, toting an assault rifle. She shielded Marcus' body and eyed up the man as he crept closer. Her heart was beating out her chest, and you could see the rhythm pulsating into her neck.

"What are you doing in here?" There was no response from the male, and he continued advancing. "There are about ten more of us inside here, so you better leave now before I call them down." The man ignored her bluff and looked past her towards the bloody body she was attempting to hide. She broke down in tears, knowing she could possibly face the same fate she just avoided outside. Her boyfriend was unable to protect her this time, and she possessed no self-defense skills. She backed up once more, in an effort to keep a good amount of distance between herself and the armed man. As she stepped back, she felt cold metal pressed against her heel. *That could be a pipe*, she thought to herself. She quickly reached down to grab the object, hoping it would deter the potential attacker. Once lifted, the man stopped in his tracks and raised his rifle. She noticed his aggressive gesture and held the object in front of her, noticing it was the shotgun that Marcus took from the thugs. She readjusted her grip and now had the gun aimed at her new target. A sudden surge of fear ran through her body as she attempted to get a strong grip on the gun she was very unfamiliar with. Her arms shook because she had never been in this type of situation before and couldn't imagine taking someone's life. The man noticed how jittery she was and began to chuckle.

Naturally, she became confused and felt it was odd for a thug to find humor in her obvious lack of experience when it came to handling a shotgun. His laughter made her angrier because the situation she was currently in was not funny and her life was not a joking matter.

"What the fuck do you want?" she snarled, as tears began flowing from her eyes.

"Stitches," he replied.

"What?"

"Stitches. He's going to need stitches." The man lowered his gun and pointed towards Marcus.

She looked back and noticed the blood continually pouring from the laceration on Marcus' head. He was in really bad shape. Just as quickly as she looked at Marcus, the man had disarmed her and had the barrel of the shotgun pressed against her neck. She had enough and closed her eyes to accept her fate. She deserved to die since she didn't have the guts to pull the trigger. She let Marcus down, and she knew it.

"This is why I was laughing," the man said as she chuckled again. "I knew as soon as you picked it up you weren't going to do shit with it."

She ignored his attempt at friendly banter and turned her head to the side. It seemed that her luck had run out and fate wanted to take its place. The feeling of cold steel pressed against her neck had suddenly diminished, and she opened one eye to see why. To her surprise, the man had kneeled down over Marcus and was cleaning his wounds with the supplies she brought down. He clearly knew what he was doing, seeing as though he was very precise in the manner he used each supply.

"I'm going to need a needle and some thread. Oh and a lighter if you have one."

"What are you a doctor or something?"

He ignored the irrelevant question and continued cleaning the wound. She ran upstairs to gather the materials, the man requested. Luckily, they had each item stocked in the house. She handed him the items, along with a cigar from Marcus' collection. It was like a peace offering between the two, seeing as though they had a standoff off moments before. He grabbed the cigar and smiled, accepting the gracious gift. Marcus was still knocked out cold, and the man wanted to get the wounds patched up before they became infected. Once the head wound was clean, he set the needle over the open flame from the lighter. He pinched the wound and began stitching. He noticed the one-woman audience that hovered over him, watching his every move. Once he was satisfied with his work, he whipped out a large serrated pocket knife. With one swoop, he sliced Marcus' shirt off. "Help me turn him over," he instructed. They both grabbed Marcus and leaned him on his side, revealing the horrendous wounds on his back. "They look bad, but I think they are just superficial. I will clean and dress them,' the man said to deaf ears because she was looking away in disgust at the ripped flesh on her boyfriend's bloody back. He grabbed the rubbing alcohol and poured the entire bottle onto the wounds. It was a good thing Marcus was passed out because that would have surely been an agonizing experience. He let that sit for about ninety seconds before pouring a bottle of hydrogen peroxide over the wounds. The foaming effect ensured him the chemical was doing its job. He performed those same tasks once again to ensure each inch of the wounds had been doused.

"What the hell am I going to do with this?" he asked sarcastically, holding up a small tube of Neosporin. She looked over at him and giggled, which took her mind off the bad episode of ER she was currently starring in.

"Well, that's all we have."

"I need much more than this."

"Oh, so what am I supposed to go run to the store and get some? Must I remind you that I almost died an hour ago?" Sarcasm had filled the air, along with the stench of blood, flesh, and rubbing alcohol.

"Do you have Vaseline?"

"I think we do."

"Well go get me that, a spatula and some plastic wrap if you have some."

Upon receiving the next set of orders, she ran upstairs briefly and back down into the kitchen. Returning about five minutes after her little scavenger hunt, she dropped a slew of items next to the man. He now had the items he requested along with two jars of Aquaphor ointment and a bottle of Amsterdam Vodka. "Since you keep bringing back gifts, how 'bout some steak and potatoes on the next run?" he grinned as she burst out into laughter.

"Hey, I thought you might like it."

"We'll see, I'm a whiskey guy. Hey, do me a favor and mix the Vaseline, Aquaphor, and Neosporin for me. Use the spatula."

She followed the orders to a tee and made a concoction that the man applied smoothly across Marcus' back with the spatula. Once again, his audience was locked in as he dressed the wounds and covered them with the plastic wrap. "Where did you learn how to do all of this?"

"The military."

"Are you the one that shot that guy outside?"

"Yeah. My name is Kyle, and you are?"

"Candice. I am Candice, and that is my boyfriend, Marcus. Thank you so much for helping us."

CHAPTER

9

"**Oh gosh. I'm so** nervous. Whose decision was it for me to meet your parents?

Sitting on the edge of their bed, Marcus stared at Candice who was trying to find the perfect outfit to wear to dinner. Her words were going in one ear and out the other. She had always been reluctant about meeting Marcus' parents because she remembered the horror stories he told her about his mother running off his prior ex-girlfriends. Between the large pile of clothes on the bed and the pile at her feet, Candice could open her own thrift shop and make millions.

"Bae, they are going to love you just like I do."

"How are you so sure?"

"I just know."

"Well did you tell them I was white?"

Marcus knew this question was coming. He let out a deep sigh because he knew he was entering into a conversation that they had hundreds of times. Race *played a big issue in their relationship, seeing as though interracial relationships were such a big issue in society. It took them a while to find the perfect apartment because Marcus felt uncomfortable in the ritzy white neighborhoods and Candice felt unaccepted in middle-class black neighborhoods. Luckily, the rental house they found was in a very diverse neighborhood and they never had any issues. Nevertheless, that did not stop their families from giving them problems, particularly Candice's father. He was very inappropriate with Marcus during their first meet at Candice's college graduation a year ago. Making statements such as "I guess you didn't go to college," when he saw Marcus sitting in the audience and not amongst the graduates. He was surprised to hear Marcus had graduated two years prior with high honors and now had a successful career as an engineer. Next came "So did you play basketball for the school?" and "Did your parents attend college?" Marcus did not appreciate the inappropriate questioning, but he was a gentleman and remained respectful to her parents. Now, their relationship has grown tremendously, and he isn't questioned as much when he sees her father.*

"Of course I told my parents you are white. I'm not a fan of the element of surprise like you."

Candice rolled her eyes and posed in front of their full-length mirror. She pinned up her blonde hair and admired her new rose tattoo. It was still fresh, so she had a glob of Aquaphor, spread across it. She was finally satisfied with the floral top and white jeans she was sporting as she pranced around the room. She opened the closet, which concealed over sixty pairs of shoes and began rummaging through each of them. "I'm just saying I want things to be perfect. I don't want your mom to try and run me off like she did the rest."

"Listen, if you're treating me good you won't have that problem. Now if you do wrong by me, momma might kill your ass," he said trying to hold back his laughter.

Candice frowned hard. "See that's what I'm talking about, you think it's funny, and it's not."

Marcus stood up and wrapped his strong muscular arms around her thin frame and lifted her off her feet. He knew this was her weakness. Candice loved when he picked her up and held her because it made her feel secure. She turned her head back and kissed her chocolate lover on his soft lips. He turned her around, and she was now straddling him, with her arms wrapped around his neck for stability. His grip was firm, and her body was locked against his. Not even a gust of wind could pass through their snug union.

"I feel so safe in your arms," she whispered, resting her head on his broad shoulder.

"You are safe bae, I will always protect you," Marcus replied. He leaned in to steal another kiss from the love of his life. He stared into her blue eyes, and for a second they forgot about all of their worries. It was just them, and no one else existed on the planet. They locked lips again, this time more intimate as their tongues intertwined and worked their way down each other's throats. Marcus carefully placed Candice on the bed and kissed her neck.

"But what about —, what about dinner with your parents?" she asked, trying to stay strong while Marcus began licking on her neck. Her concerns about meeting his parents slowly began to fade into the back of her mind.

"We can be late," he said while he snickered. In the back of his mind, he knew that once he started making love to her, he had no intentions of stopping to get to the restaurant.

"Oh great, now your mom is really going to hate me." She laughed before letting out a loud moan as he worked his way to her ear lobe.

"Ok, I will be quick so we can make it there on time."

The couple quickly removed their clothing and Candice wrapped her legs around Marcus, to keep his body pressed up against hers. She ran her hands across his wavy hair and down his cheek, before bringing his face into hers for more kisses.

"Promise me you will always be here to protect me."

"I promise bae," Marcus muttered as he began to make love to her.

CHAPTER
10

Marcus slowly opened his eyes to awaken from a horrifying nightmare. He dreamt he was attacked outside his home. Sweat beads quickly turned to waterfalls. To his surprise, the setting he woke up in was familiar; it was his living room. As he tried to sit up, he felt an excruciating pain coming from his back and his head was throbbing. "Ah shit," he yelled out as the pain became worse once he sat back on the couch he was on.

"Take those pills next to you."

The sound of Kyle's voice startled him, as he looked over to see an unknown man armed with a rifle peeking through the blinds at the front window. "Who the fuck are you?" Marcus asked, attempting to scooch away from Kyle. "Ah fuck," he howled as he began grimacing in more pain.

"Listen, man, take those pills because your body is fucked up right now."

Marcus looked over at the three white pills that rested next to a tall glass of orange juice. He was reluctant to take them because he had no idea what they were or who Kyle was. Kyle noticed the reluctance immediately and continued to focus on the street. "It's only Excedrin asshole. We couldn't find anything stronger, so I just slid you an extra dosage."

We? Marcus thought, quickly surveying the room for an accomplice.

"Baby, you're up," Candice yelled as she ran over to him and gave him the tightest hug she could imagine. The pain was unbearable, so he had to push her off quickly. 'Oh my, I'm so sorry. I'm so happy you are awake, I was so worried that you were going to die on me."

Marcus slowly realized the nightmare he woke up from was actually reality. He had a ton of questions, but he could not help but stare into Candice's blue eyes. They left him speechless, appreciative to be alive.

"Here take your pills," she instructed.

He looked over at Kyle, who was still focused on the exterior setting. He didn't know the disciplined soldier had glanced over at the earlier encounter, which made him reminisce about his deceased family. His eyes were focused outside, but his mind was on Jacqui and Chloe. He missed his family so much but knew he had to stay strong in order to survive in this new world. Marcus took the pills and gulped down the entire glass of orange juice. He looked back over at Kyle who was still focused at the window but was now grinning.

What the hell is he smiling at? Marcus thought. He wondered what Kyle's connection was to Candice "What's his deal?" he asked Candice, trying to be discrete so Kyle wouldn't know he was inquiring about him.

"Oh, that's Kyle babe. He's the one that killed that skinny asshole from last night," she yelled out. She was so excited to finally introduce the two men.

Both men looked at each other and exchanged friendly head nods. Kyle finally stood up and grabbed a bag that was on the floor. He reached in and grabbed a jar of peanut butter. He handed the jar to Marcus and regained his position at the window. The last thing he wanted was a group of thugs or one of the creatures to creep up on them.

"How did you find us, Kyle?" Marcus somehow was able to mutter out the question in between stuffing his face with the expired, crunchy peanut butter.

"Your little girlfriend here was making so much noise in the damn house, and it interrupted what I was doing. I was able to get some weapons and ammo off those fools that tried to kill you, and I knew you would be dead if someone heard you guys inside. You were in pretty bad shape dude." Kyle looked Marcus up and down and laughed, "Well you still are I guess."

Marcus chuckled as he was introduced to Kyle's wittiness and sense of humor. Little did he know how much pain was hidden behind all that humor. "Well man, I am grateful and truly indebted to you. You saved our lives."

"Speaking of that, what was up with you and those guys last night?"

"Stupidity, that's what happened. With all the nonsense going on with the government, I figured I'd keep a little humanity going. The skinny dude knocked on the door, claiming his van broke down and I opened up to offer my assistance. As soon as I opened the door, the big guy clocked me over the head with something. Everything else is a blur. I can't believe I let my guard down like that."

"That was the scariest moment of my life. I don't know what has gotten into people, but we won't be doing that again," Candice said, chiming in on the conversation.

"Once again man, I want to thank you. If you hadn't come along, we definitely wouldn't be here having this conversation. Once I get better, I'm gon' to have Candice whip us up a nice meal, and we are gon' kick it."

"Why didn't yall evacuate like everybody else?"

Marcus hung his head low before answering. "Stupidity once again. I honestly thought this was one of those dramatic moments in U.S. history to scare everyone. They did it with the Zika virus and Ebola, so once they mentioned this other virus or whatever it is, I figured it was just to have everyone panicking. I didn't expect the bullshit from last night."

"Trust me; I know the feeling. My family begged me to leave, and I stayed like a fool."

"Your family, where are they?" asked Candice. The excitement in her voice was noticeable. She felt there would be strength in numbers and if they were anything like Kyle, they would definitely be strong.

Kyle didn't answer and turned his attention back to the minivans that blocked the street and the two bodies that lay nearby. A grave reminder of the dangers that lurked beyond their little safe haven. Marcus immediately noticed Kyle's reaction and gave Candice a piercing stare. The last thing he wanted to do was strike a nerve and push Kyle away because they asked too many of the wrong questions. Suddenly there was an awkward silence in the room.

Sweat beads were starting to form on Kyle's forehead, as the summer heat began to reveal itself inside the home. Seeing as though the energy resources were nonexistent, he wiped his forehead with his wrist. Kyle reached down and grabbed the lukewarm bottle of water that was on the floor next to him.

THUD!

The loud noise startled the group and Kyle went right back to the window. He glanced around, but could not determine where the noise came from. *Maybe it's just people in their homes trying to gather material or maybe some thugs ransacking a place.* The streets remained silent. Everything appeared in the chaotic order it was in, sixty seconds prior. There was no movement at the row of homes on the Southside of the block, the vans were still in the street, and the bodies were still on the —. THE BODIES WERE GONE. Kyle jumped up and warned the others of the new discovery. They continued looking out the window, hoping the bodies would reappear.

"Where the fuck did the bodies go?" Kyle blurted out in total confusion.

"Maybe it was that werewolf I saw," Candice stated to Marcus.

"Come on Candice, please don't start with that again. Especially not in front of other people." Marcus replied.

"Werewolf?" Kyle asked.

Candice walked over to the window and pointed out the house directly across the street from theirs. "It was in that blue house right there." Kyle peeked through the blinds at the home she was referring to. It did not appear out of place besides the obliterated front door and a few broken windows. The distance from the vans to the home had to be around twenty to thirty feet, so it would not take much for someone or something to drag the bodies inside without being seen.

"Listen, Kyle, there are no werewolves out there. Candice was just trippin' that night. She's crazy."

"Oh she isn't crazy. Trust me, it might not be werewolves but there are definitely some types of beasts roaming around."

CHAPTER 11

THE BLACK DODGE DURANGO turned the corner like a bat out of hell and pulled up on the abandoned street. Music was blaring through the speakers, and the odor of burnt rubber polluted the air. The drunk driver parked his vehicle like a true professional. He was proud of his accomplishment: not tapping the cars in front or behind him during the parallel parking attempt.

"Marcus, I can't believe we just did that. That was so much fun."

"Bae, I told you nobody would be around. Everyone left, so I knew there would be no one at the bar and we needed to get out of the house."

Candice jumped on Marcus' back and requested a piggyback ride. Her short skirt rose up during her leap, exposing her lace panties and firm rear end. He secured her legs by wrapping his arms around them and gave her the ride of a lifetime, fifty feet to the front *door of the house. He struggled to find the key to the front door and attempted several others before dropping the bunch on the top step. Marcus bent over to get the keys. Candice was still on his back, and his current movements exposed her goods once again. When he bent over, her glassy eyes caught a glimpse of a minivan parking at the end of the street. At one o'clock in the morning, it was odd to see anyone else out. Candice unsaddled her stallion and tried to be discreet about her new sighting. She remembered the warnings the government put out about criminals roaming the streets at night, but thought they were all wiped out during the gassings.*

"Hurry up and get the door open, there is someone up the street."

Marcus looked both ways in an attempt to see what Candice was so nervous about, but in his current condition could barely see the keys that were in front of his face. That is exactly what happens when you start downing bottles of Patron as if they are Aquafina. The longer they stood on the front porch, the more vulnerable Candice felt. "Here let me do it," she said as she snatched the keys from Marcus' hand. He was still twiddling his thumbs as if the set of keys were still in his hand. Candice finally got the door unlocked and wasted no time entering the home. Marcus immediately face-planted on the couch, while Candice secured the home. Seeing the minivan parked at the end of the street immediately sobered her up, and she could not keep her mind off it. Who the hell was in that van? Did they follow us home from the bar? How long are they going to sit out there?

Candice's thoughts left her somewhat paranoid as she worked her way to the upstairs bedroom. She opened the window and sat at it, waiting to see what the van was going to do. With all the lights blacked out in the house, she had a great vantage point on the entire block. It was quiet besides the soft sound of an engine running idle. Time was ticking away, and there still wasn't any movement from the silver minivan. Candice occasionally glanced over at the clock on the nightstand. Thirty minutes went by, and there was still no movement. The cool breeze flowed through the window like central air, and it was just enough to make Candice doze off.

HOWL. HOWL. HOWL.

The high-pitched sound woke Candice up from an unexpected slumber. The clock now read five o'clock and the morning breeze was warming up. Candice surveyed the area from the discreet position, and the streets were still quiet. That was until another howl echoed through the air. It came from across the street. *The McBurns,* she thought when she realized one of the homes on the block had fresh damage. The front door was demolished as if a SWAT team hit it and the glass from several windows was completely busted out. Candice looked up and down the street, in search of the silver van, but it was nowhere in sight. *Those fuckers probably did this.* Another howl grabbed Candice's attention once more. It was much louder than a dog's and they did not live in Alaska, so she was sure it *wasn't a wolf. Her eyes widened, mouth dropped to the floor, and body froze in place.*

First seeing the large snout of the beast, she could not believe what was emerging from the front doorway of the McBurns residence. Its sharp claws dug into the concrete like a small jackhammer, as it crawled out on all fours. Muscles protruded from its back as it rose up and stood on its hind legs, displaying the chiseled muscles on its abdomen. "Oh shit a fuckin' werewolf," Candice whispered to herself. The beast's head turned in her direction, and its red pupils targeted her corner in the window. "Fuck." The beast seemed to hear that quiet outburst as well. Digging into the ground, it stepped forward and began growling at Candice. The sharp daggers in its mouth were enough to free her from her paralysis as she made her way down the steps. She jumped on top of Marcus, who was still feeling the effects of last night's rendezvous.

"Babe it's a werewolf outside, get up. Get the hell up." Marcus grumbled and turned over, the alcohol still dispersing from his pores. "Marcus, wake up." Candice shook his body violently, but that had little to no effect on the man that was clearly in a drunken hibernation. Candice ran towards the front door, slamming her palms on the strong wood to prevent herself from running through it. She peeked through the peephole to confirm the earlier visual. She wanted to make sure the beast was still on the front step of the McBurns residence. As she peeked through, Candice saw nothing. She could not even see the houses across

the street, which was odd. Peering into darkness concerned her.

With her face pressed against the door, Candice could hear a loud panting coming from the other side. Her stomach dropped, and she slowly crept away from the door. The panting slowly turned to scratching and Candice was now back by Marcus' side. Trying not to make a lot of noise, she began shaking Marcus again. His deep snoring was an indicator that her efforts went in vain. The scratching stopped, and Candice was able to regain her composure. She remembered the set of knives Marcus put in the closet to defend against intruders. He definitely wasn't referring to four-legged beasts, but it was better than nothing. Candice started making her way to the closet when the doorknob began rattling. She let out a loud scream that could have woken every neighbor in a ten-block radius.

Marcus jumped up from the light coma and stumbled over to Candice. "Candy what's wrong? What happened?" The stench of tequila smacked her in the face.

She stood in place, shaking from head to toe. Her index finger was pointing at the front door that was ironically unbothered at the moment. Marcus looked at her, and then looked at the door. "Did someone try to come in here?" Still no response from his lover, who was now turning pale. He walked over to the door to see what all the commotion was about. He looked through the peephole for a second before turning the key and unlocking the door.

"No Marcus don't fuckin' open that door."

"Why not? I don't see anyone out here."

"A were—. A were—wolf."

"A what?" Marcus burst out in laughter. Unable to control himself, he was almost in tears. "You can't be serious bae. A werewolf in our neighborhood? You really have to stop watching all that Twilight shit; it has you going crazy. Ain't no damn werewolf out here." Marcus unlocked the door and began turning the knob. Candice ran over to the closet and armed herself with two steak knives, anticipating the worst. Marcus flung the door open, and Candice positioned herself out of sight of the beast. Rays from the rising sun shined through the front door, and the light breeze worked its way in. "See, I told you no one was out here."

Candice peeked out from the corner and saw that the howling beast had not devoured her boyfriend. She walked to the front door and looked out. The streets seemed undisturbed and quiet. The sound of birds chirping was much more delightful than the howling of the beast that she was now skeptical of seeing. *Maybe I had too much to drink last night.* Candice walked to the edge of the front porch and stared at the damaged McBurns residence. Pieces of the front door dangled from the hinges and shattered glass was strewn all over the front yard. Despite the sun rising, there was complete darkness in the home. Candice was expecting the beast to emerge from the black abyss. After realizing, her mind was playing tricks on her she walked back towards the house.

"*No more liquor for you, you're going crazy,*" *Marcus muttered.*

Candice ignored his ignorant comment and brushed by him to walk in the house. As she did, her shirt snagged on a protruding piece of wood. Oh great, what else could go wrong. She looked and noticed several deep scratches on the surface of the front door and around the knob. I KNEW IT.

CHAPTER 12

"**HOW MUCH FURTHER ARE** we going to walk?" Candice asked, leaning on a fire hydrant to give her legs a slight break. The group had spent days making their way through different neighborhoods, in search of civilization. On some streets, the orange fog was so thick you could not see your hand even if it was held up in front of your face. Their gas masks were the only protection against the deadly chemical. It was a good thing Kyle brought along the extra two. Luckily, the masks only needed to be worn through the thick fog; once the air appeared clear, there were no immediate effects if breathed in. Kyle figured this out by spending a significant amount of time watching one of the blocks on the first day of their excursion. Although he did not know when the gas was disseminated, it took a little over four hours for it to disperse in the air. It started out as smoke rising to the sky, and after two hours lingered in the air like a fog. This gave him an idea of how long they could expect to keep the masks on if they encountered the militia again and the gas canisters were used against them. The air quality was the least of the group's problem. Kyle knew they would not last long on the minimum food supply they had. The group managed to forage food on their journey, but most of it was expired. Old cans of baked beans, fruit cocktail, and peanut butter filled their bags. Kyle never mentioned his small stash of MREs. They would only be consumed in dire emergencies. Marcus even took it as far as to cut away moldy portions of bread and eat the remainder of the slices. They also had to worry about the thugs and beasts that wouldn't hesitate to kill each and every one of them, when the opportunity presented itself. On their journey, they scavenged through different homes and were able to shelter in place from inclement weather.

"Over here," Marcus yelled out as he forced open the front door to an old row home. Although the home appeared outdated, it was one of the only homes on the block that wasn't exposed due to shattered windows or missing doors. Kyle was the first to enter the home with the barrel of his Springfield Saint leading the way. He cleared the living room and dining room, which was unoccupied. Kyle signaled for Marcus and Candice to take the second floor. Marcus was the first up the stairs, with a nine-millimeter Ruger he found in the trunk of an abandoned car. Candice followed behind with a steak knife. Despite being almost raped and murdered, she still had an innocence about her. It was something about guns that made her uncomfortable, so she refused to take one of Kyle's many handguns.

"Looks like someone's already been through here," Marcus announced after noticing the jewelry box, safe and closets had all been emptied.

Candice was in another bedroom and discovered a large pile of empty shell casings and gas canisters. She crept into the remaining bedroom, while Marcus checked the bathroom in the hallway. *Who the hell was in here*, Candice thought as she peeked under the bed and inside the closet. The bedroom was cleared, but Candice noticed Marcus was still in the bathroom. She walked by and saw him kneeling down towards an air vent.

"What is it?" she asked.

He raised his hand but didn't say a word. Candice stayed quiet and allowed her eyes to explore the bathroom, wondering what required her boyfriend's immediate attention. Marcus didn't change his position and remained in front of the vent. CLANK! CLANK! The soft sound of a banging pipe traveled up the vent, which caught Marcus' attention. The clanking suddenly stopped, and the two decided to run downstairs to notify Kyle.

"Yo Kyle," Marcus yelled out as he ran down the stairs. "There's a noise coming from the —"

Kyle was holding his index finger up to his lip. Marcus didn't say another word and slowly approached him. He was posted in front of a door in the kitchen. He knocked on the door three times and looked at the other two. CLANK! CLANK! CLANK! The sound of the banging pipe was louder and clearly coming from behind the door. Marcus immediately raised his gun, letting Kyle know he was ready for whatever surprise was waiting for them behind the door.

"Candice come here," Kyle whispered. "On three, I want you to pull the door open."

Candice nodded and placed her shaking hand on the doorknob. The rattling from the knob revealed the current state of her nerves. She was shaking uncontrollably and could not help it. Opening the door could have unleashed a number of dangers, especially knowing someone had recently been in the home before them. In the back of Candice's mind, she always flashes back to the night she was almost taken from Marcus and thinks about the type of evil that is roaming the streets. Back when the country was in order, you would be able to call the police and let them deal with criminals, but now the responsibility falling on each individual citizen was hard to cope with. Her deep, blue eyes were locked on Kyle as she waited for his signal.

"Now," he whispered as he watched her pull the door towards her body. His rifle was up, as he inched towards the opening. Cutting each angle like a pie, Kyle was able to safely get a view of what was behind the door. A set of rickety steps led down to a dark basement. The strong stench of blood and flesh overpowered Kyle's nostrils. He knew the putrid odor immediately, which is that of a rotting body. He ran into this familiar odor plenty of times, back when his unit would clear homes and find houses full of Iraqi citizens that had been victims of terrorist attacks. Their rotting corpses would bake in the house like an oven, and once the door was opened, the aroma of death attacked your sense of smell. Kyle carefully shined his flashlight down into the basement, but could not spot anything but old clothes thrown about the floor. He would have to go into the basement to investigate the suspicious clanking noise but wanted to make sure the others were comfortable in doing so.

A surge ran through Marcus' gut, causing him to tumble towards the kitchen wall. He folded over at the waist and placed his hand over his mouth, attempting to stop the contents of his stomach from exiting. He was not used to the smell of death, and his reaction clearly showed it. Vomit seeped through the spacing between his fingers and suddenly exploded out his mouth. A combination of expired baked beans, moldy bread, and canned fruit cocktail coated the kitchen floor. Kyle looked over at Marcus who was bent over at the waist. If they were in the home alone, he would have burst out in laughter at the site of Marcus puking his brains out, but he was currently on a mission. It seemed a tad bit too quiet in the basement, which made the hairs on the back of Kyle's neck stand up. The first step he took down the basements steps let out a loud creak, which could be heard on the top floor of the house. Each subsequent step followed suit, just barely sturdy enough to support his weight.

ARRGGHH!

It was massive with glaring red eyes that seemed to be looking through Kyle. It held in its sharp claws a thing that had once been a man, gnawing at the head as if it were a stick of sugar cane with sweet juices emerging from the flesh. "What the fuck," Kyle subconsciously muttered, as he watched the creature devour what was left of the human corpse it had been feasting on. Its position was kind of slumped over to its right side, and Kyle noticed a gaping wound on the beast's right leg. The injury obviously didn't stop it from partaking in what could have possibly been its last meal. Pieces of a shotgun were sprawled about the basement floor. Only that weapon could have inflicted that type of damage to the beast at such a close range. Kyle just assumed the entrée the beast recently consumed was possibly the shooter. What struck him as odd was the lack of the beast's concern of his presence. He felt that at the moment he emerged from the stairs, it should have dropped its present prey and sought out the fresh morsel that stood amongst it. But for some reason, both man and beast did nothing more but carefully observe each other. The creaking from the steps served as a diversion. The dogface of the beast turned away from Kyle and towards the feet that were cautiously stepping down into its domain. CLANK! CLANK! CLANK! The sound of the metal chain dragging against the water pipe it was affixed to, confirmed that the beast made the noise that caught the scavengers attention. The chain was tied around its next and was the only thing, besides its injury, which prevented it from advancing towards Kyle. With its pointed ears, dark fur, bloodshot eyes, wet nose, sharp teeth, and blood-covered lips, it stopped Candice in her tracks.

"The werewolf," she muttered, recognizing the similar features it had to the beast that clawed at her front door.

The beast watched Candice intently, as she sidestepped towards Kyle. She had a tight grip on her knife but knew there was no way she was getting close to the creature that sat in front of her. It would be no different from wrestling with a grizzly bear since the beast was identical in size. Candice looked over and noticed Kyle hadn't said a word or blinked. His rifle was down by his side when she would rather have him pointing it at the beast. She nudged his arm, in an attempt to disrupt him from his current state of temporary paralysis, but it was to no avail. Kyle's attention was fully on the beast, which now appeared to be relaxing. It's furry head rested on the ground, next to the remains of its meal. There was no concern about the two people that were watching it. Even when Marcus emerged down the creaking steps, the beast did not move. Marcus didn't last long in the basement because once he glanced over at the human remains left by the beast, the remaining contents that once sat in his stomach erupted from his mouth and sent him running back upstairs.

CHAPTER 13

"**Star, they are still** in the house."

It had been hours since he watched the three enter the home across the street. A gust of wind pushed the curtain to the side, as cool air entered the room. He dug his dirty fingers in the can of chicken noodle soup he had cooling on the floor. Using his index finger to stir the soup, it was the right temperature for consumption. Using a lighter to heat up the soup was a method he had not tried before, but it seemed to be effective. Ignoring the dirt particles that floated at the top of the soup, he placed the rim of the warm can against his crusty lips and sipped on the warm soup. It had been weeks since he had anything other than cold cans of mixed vegetables to eat, so the warm sensation that filled his belly was almost euphoric.

"Oh my gosh Star, this is like heaven in a can. Do you want some?" He poured the remaining contents of the can into his partner's mouth. She wasted no time consuming the tender noodles and salty broth. "You had a long day girl, try to get some rest." His hand rubbed his best friend's back, but his eyes were focused on the movements he observed across the street. The cool breeze against his face was enough to put him to sleep, and that is exactly what his body yearned for.

THUD! THUD!

"Oh Star, it looks like our guest wants something. I'm going to go see what the bastard wants." Being lazy, he used the AK-47 assault rifle he was holding as a crutch to stand from his crouched position. He sashayed to the back room, with the rifle dangling from its shoulder strap. The flamboyant man was not one you would expect to handle such a powerful weapon, but he was not naïve to the damage an AK-47 could cause. THUD! The sound of a woman banging her head against the headboard annoyed him greatly. This was going to be her third warning not to make any noise, but clearly her only concern was being disobedient. She watched him walk towards her. Wearing a small, pink t-shirt, a pair of gray H&M skinny jeans, and white Jordan sneakers, she could not believe he held her fate in his hand. Cursing him out was pointless because he placed a sock in her mouth and wrapped duct tape around her face to secure it. She wanted to rip his head off but unfortunately, her arms were tied to the bedposts.

"Listen, honey, I told you to stop making noise in here," he said as he ran the barrel of the AK across her stomach. She flinched as the cool metal glided across her bare skin. She was only wearing a bra and panties since the feminine man that stood before her was now sporting her outfit. He didn't even have the decency to give her the old clothes he was wearing or something out of a closet from the home they were in. He placed the AK down on the bed, at her feet.

"I have a surprise for you darling. I'm going to make you look beautiful," he said while admiring the brown-haired woman's natural beauty. Unzipping the pink fanny pack around his waist, he removed several cosmetics and placed them on her stomach. Using her body as his own personal workstation, he sorted the products and began dolling her up. He began singing the lyrics to *Run the World (Girls) by Beyonce* and started applying primer to her face. His touch made her skin crawl while on the other end, he was mesmerized by her soft skin. "This is how they made me. Houston, Texas baby," he sang as he brushed concealer across her forehead and chin. He was delicate when applying the foundation and highlights. "Who run this motherfucker, who run this motherfucker," he continued singing. He stood up and began dancing to the tune in his head, occasionally glancing over and admiring his work. Tears began to form in her eyes as he applied eyeliner and mascara. He was not bothered by the fact it was running down her cheeks. Reaching back into the fanny pack and pushing items aside, he finally found what he was looking for. The delightful scent of Daisy by Marc Jacobs filled his nose, as he rubbed the perfume stick across her neck. He slowly leaned into her neck, which caused goose bumps to rise on her body. With a deep inhale, he sniffed the strong aroma until the smell was trapped in his nostrils. "Last but not least my dear," the man muttered as he slowly applied the bright, red Revlon lipstick to his own lips. He leaned in slowly for a kiss, but she abruptly turned her head, which left her cheek exposed for the soft pucker. He sat back and laughed at the woman's gesture. "You are such a bitch," he snarled before gathering his cosmetics and returning them to the fanny pack. "But don't worry you will be the most beautiful bitch ever to cross the gates of hell." He slung the AK over his shoulder and opened the closet door.

While backpedaling, he slid open the mirrored closet door and watched as a beast emerged from the darkness. It was relatively small and would be considered a cub if it were another animal. A metal chain was wrapped around its neck and affixed to the metal closet rod. The beast initially locked eyes on the man that let it free and began advancing. He raised the AK and continued backpedaling until he was in the threshold. The little beast continued advancing until the slack was out the chain and it could no longer close the distance between itself and the prize it had its eye on. The small brown-haired beast began sniffing the floor. Drool dripped from its little fangs, and its claws tore the carpet as it stepped towards the bed. It continued sniffing until it got to the woman's leg. Ironically, the chain was long enough for the beast to reach the tied up woman. Once she saw the creature mounting her, she squirmed like a fish but nothing she did loosened the restraints on her ankles and wrists. The beast took a chunk out of her arm as it plunged forward for the first bite. Despite her mouth being covered, the woman's shriek could be heard as it slightly escaped the duct tape. Blood trickled down, and pain shot through her arm, as the beast feasted on her body. The male walked out and closed the bedroom door behind him. A devilish grin ran from ear to ear.

CHAPTER 14

"**OK NOW SOMEONE NEEDS** to tell me what the fuck that thing in the basement is," Marcus yelled. He paced back and forth in the living room. Kyle and Candice sat on the couch, chuckling at Marcus' dramatic reaction. He vomited approximately four times, and the odor still lurked from the kitchen. His concern about the situation became their amusement for the night.

"What the fuck are yall laughing at?"

"Yo man, calm down," Kyle replied, noticing the frustration on Marcus' face.

"Calm down? You want me to calm fuckin' down? There is a fuckin' monster tied up in the fuckin' basement, and you want me to calm down."

"It's a werewolf," Candice said, as she couldn't hold back her laughter any longer. Kyle joined along in the laughter, and it sent Marcus over the edge.

"What the fuck," he screamed. "They think this is a fuckin' joke." He stormed into the kitchen, stepping over his puddle of vomit and began digging through the refrigerator.

"That thing down there is scary. I mean it was scary before, but up close it is terrifying," Candice stated. "Was it like that the first time you saw it?"

"Not really," Kyle replied.

"What? What's that supposed to mean?"

"The first time I saw one of those things, it was let out of the back of a U-Haul truck. It sort of looked the same with all the fur, but it moved differently. It walked on two feet and supported itself with its hands, like an ape, and that thing down there was on all fours like a dog."

"Oh great, so there are different types of those things out here," Marcus chimed in from the kitchen.

"I have no idea. It definitely looks the same, but the movements and mannerisms weren't the same at all. That thing down there didn't even try to attack us."

"Yeah because it was all tied up. I bet if it wasn't, it would have had all of us for dessert," Marcus said. "And speaking of being tied up, who the hell do you think put that big ass monster in the basement?"

"Probably the same people that left all that crap upstairs," Candice replied, referring to her findings in the upstairs bedrooms.

"What crap?" Kyle inquired.

Candice led Kyle and Marcus up to the bedroom where she found the shell casings. Kyle immediately noticed the large pile of empty casings on the ground and began going through them. With a handful of the differently sized casings, he meticulously went through the mixture of the rifle, shotgun, and handgun casings. "Forty cal, two-two-three, shotgun slugs and AK forty-seven rounds," he mumbled while conducting his inventory. He also noticed a pile full of live rounds and gas canisters that were in close proximity to his current location in the room. Candice didn't know the difference between live and spent rounds, so she never collected the live rounds. Kyle wasted no time stuffing his duffel bag with the discarded ammunition.

"What are these for?" Marcus asked, holding up a few canisters that were also discarded.

Kyle grabbed one from him and examined it. An identical match to the canister that was thrown into his home. He knew the metal housing once contained the deadly chemical gas, but couldn't figure out why the housings and ammo were in this particular home. "These are the canisters the gas is stored in," he informed the two.

"Well I think it's some still in this one," Marcus replied. He noticed a distinguishable difference in the weight of the two canisters that were in his hand.

"This one feels like something is in it," Candice stated as she checked the weight differences of the remaining canisters on the floor.

The full canisters were placed into the duffel bag with the ammo, and there was chatter about what they could do with that type of chemical weapon. Kyle was more focused on why the weapons were in the house and why things were left behind. *Who the hell brought this shit up here*, he thought as his eyes scanned the empty casings. The casings were directly under the window, and that was next to be scanned by the trained eyes of the former Marine. Bullet holes decorated the area around the window frame and shattered glass was hidden beneath the casings. Kyle pulled the curtain back slightly and peeked out the window, being careful not to expose himself too much. He scanned the exterior of the property, which was an alleyway that ran behind the home. Suddenly he raised his rifle and aimed directly outside, below the window.

CHAPTER 15

"**WELL, HE NEEDS TO** stop acting like a bitch and learn how to defend himself."

"Why do you always put your son down Howard? He needs you right now, and as a man, you should teach him how to stand up to those bullies."

Dannie sat on the steps and listened to his parents argue with each other. As usual, he was the topic of conversation. At the tender age of fifteen, he was going through an identity crisis. After his father found him prancing around in his mother's high heels, he inflicted a beating on Dannie that teetered the thin line between discipline and abuse. Since then their relationship struggled, and his father kept his distance. He spent more time at the bar all of a sudden. Dannie knew that shame kept his father from coming home at night. His mother knew it as well but tried her best to make excuses as to the whereabouts of her husband. The current issue was a group of boys at

Dannie's school that made it their purpose to make his life a living hell. Each day the bullying became worse, receiving both physical and mental abuse at home and school.

"Get your ass up and out my house," his father ordered. "Stop acting like a little girl and stand up for yourself."

Those words replayed in Dannie's mind throughout the entire morning. He did not want to go to school, but he really did not have a choice. With no friends, there was nowhere for him to go and no one to hang out with. He meandered around the neighborhood, attempting to waste time. Once his parents went to work, he would return home to relax and raid his mother's closet. The high priced heels were simply irresistible. As time ticked by, he began working his way back home. Dannie walked with his head on a swivel, hoping to avoid danger at any cost. He pictured himself twirling around in his mother's designer gowns and accessories that could compliment any outfit. Just those brief thoughts put a little joy in his heart.

"You fuckin' fag."

The words cut Dannie like a dagger. Sharp jabs to his midsection that was nothing short of agonizing. Unfortunately, he immediately recognized the voice and knew hatred like that could only come from one person. A silver Chevy Impala drove alongside him as he walked home. He never noticed the vehicle making a U-turn once the occupants spotted him. He was too caught up in fantasyland to realize the bullies he *wanted to avoid in school were driving right next to him. Dannie suddenly had a little pep in his step as he tried to get to the house as soon as possible, no matter if there was the risk that his parents would spot him.*

"Where you going you little faggot?" one of the bullies asked.

Dannie ignored the question and continued on. It was disappointing that people were witnessing the harassment, but no one did a thing about it. Simply telling the boys in the Chevy to leave Dannie alone would have been sufficient and sent the boys on their way. In his opinion, any adult watching a child being bullied is just as much of a problem as the offenders themselves. He was around the corner from his home, and the determination was evident as he was now in a soft sprint. His adrenaline was pumping, and the only sound he heard was that of his beating chest. Dannie never felt the first blow. It was a closed fist connecting with the side of his face, which knocked him off his feet. It was quickly followed up by more punches and kicks. Dannie did what he could to defend himself against the attackers, but there was not much to be done in a five-versus-one fight. Dannie kicked, scratched, and screamed as if his life depended on it and in a way, it did. The assault was brutal. Punch after punch, kick after kick. He literally felt his ribs cracking, body bruising and swelling start to form. His head bounced off the pavement as the attackers stomped on him as if he were a lit cigarette they were trying to put out. Blood leaking from his nose, mouth, and ears did not stop the attackers from introducing the sole of their Timberland boots to Dannie's face.

"Hey, you kids knock it off." The sound of an adult voice was calming. Although Dannie never had the opportunity to meet the person that interrupted the assault, he was thankful they intervened and saved his life. As he faded in and out of consciousness, he watched the Timberland boots slam on the concrete, with each step the attackers took as they fled.

Dannie stared at the pair of Timberlands that sat in the corner of the room. A slight burning smell, tickled his nostrils, as he seemed to be in a daze. He snapped back to reality and focused on the meal he was preparing. The open flame spread across the bottom of the can, and the contents came to a boil. "Star, are you ready for this? It's tomato soup. Not as good as momma used to make, but still good?" He split the soup with his friend, and there were no complaints.

Dannie reached over and opened the beach bag that contained goods he stole from across the street. He smiled as he counted at least five more cans of soup, jewelry, and ammunition. Once he spotted the jeweled statement necklace, he wasted no time placing it around his neck. He stood in front of a mirror and admired himself. The sound of a revving engine interrupted Dannie's brief moment of admiration. He crouched down and made his way over to the window. Just as he expected, the group had returned.

A small convoy pulled up, led by a tan Mercury Grand Marquis, and followed up by two U-Haul trucks and a red Jeep Liberty. When Dannie first saw the group, they arrived and left in a Ford Focus, the Mercury, and the Jeep. He looked up and down the block, but there was no sign of the Ford. The bright moon served as a spotlight on the arriving group. There was no question in Dannie's mind that the group was here to retrieve the beasts they had left behind. A day prior, he watched the group chain up the two beasts in the middle of the street and drag each of them in two separate houses. For a week, the group stayed in the two houses, while Dannie took up shelter in an abandoned car. The eighteen-year old had no one to count on but himself at the time, and of course Star. She was with him since he ran away from home five years prior. Jumping around from shelter to shelter, he had to quickly learn how to defend himself. Every chance someone got, they tested him. It wasn't until he met Adina Olusada, did he truly focus on finding himself and his purpose in life. Born of Ethiopian decent, Adina worked hard to please her parents who wanted nothing more than to see her become a doctor. She was on the right path until her sophomore year at the University of Pennsylvania when she was introduced to cocaine at a frat party she attended. The use of cocaine and a promiscuous lifestyle lead to her grades falling off and the loss of scholarships. Once her parents found out about her failing out of college, they cut off all ties to her and she was left on the streets. Navigating through the streets of Philadelphia wasn't easy for Adina. Her drug addiction grew and she ended up in a relationship with a drug dealer that continued to feed her habit. Although their small drug business was lucrative, they became targets of the Philadelphia Police Department's Narcotic Strike Force who raided their West Philadelphia home and found enough drug evidence to send them both away for years. After serving sixty-three months in the Riverside Correctional Facility, Adina bounced around shelters and met the boy that would eventually become a brother to her. Adina saw Dannie for what he truly was; a weak, lost soul that longed to be accepted. She helped him build character and self-esteem while finding his true self. He no longer had to hide behind masculinity and stopped caring about what others thought. Although Adina helped build him up mentally and emotionally, she also corrupted him by introducing him to the world of robbery and petty theft. The two of them, with the assistance of Star, would hit corner stores, banks, and other local businesses. They were good at what they did, but also sloppy and arrogant. They never wore masks or attempted to conceal their identities in any way and once the chaos in Philadelphia began, they didn't need to worry because crime became the norm.

Dannie spent a week watching the group go back and forth between the homes. He studied them and their movements. He counted a total of ten members, six men and four women. Every single one of them was armed. Gunfire erupted daily and carried over until the night hours. Occasionally he watched as they threw what appeared to be grenades in neighboring homes. Orange smoke would emanate from those same homes, and that is when Dannie discovered the creatures.

During one of the group's missions, a family of three was attacked in their home. He saw two of the men drag a woman from a house before they threw their smoke grenades inside. The woman's screams could be heard for hours at a time, as the men rotated in and out one of the safe houses. Dannie wanted to do something to help, but realistically the machete he carried around would be no match for the group's firepower. It hadn't been until twenty-four hours after the attack on the family when Dannie saw them. The orange smoke inside the house was no longer visible, but something else emerged from the house. Dannie was in total disbelief and figured the summer heat was making him delirious. In his mind, being in the compact Honda Civic for a few days, during ninety-degree weather was no different than, attempting to cross the Sahara Desert. It felt like he was taking a hot, steamy shower as the warm sweat dripped down his face and soaked his dingy wife beater. The smell of sweat and onions had gone unnoticeable to Dannie, as the stench became the normal scent in his current environment.

Dannie wiped his eyes, believing his fatigued body and mind were playing tricks on him. Two beasts emerged from the house. One was large and slowly crept out the front doorway. It was like nothing Dannie had ever laid eyes on. Behind it, another smaller beast climbed out the window. The two beasts roamed around the street, like stray dogs. It was as if they were exploring new territory. The smaller beast did not linger far behind the larger, as cubs stay in close proximity to their mothers. For some odd reason,

Dannie wasn't terrified of the creatures. They were amazing and mysterious in his eyes. He thought about the millions he would have made in the old world, with the discovery of a new animal species. Little did he know, the beasts were products of the mutation of the human race. *I wonder what they eat*, he thought as he turned on his iPhone. Dannie hoped to get a picture of the beasts for his collection. He figured someone needed to add these troubling times to American history and there needed to be proof of it all. Photographs and videos would be more than enough to make Dannie rich and famous in the new world. He always enjoyed photography, but once the camera on his battery died, he decided to periodically turn off his iPhone to preserve its battery life. The phone turned on and displayed the forty-eight percent-battery life remaining. Dannie swiped to the camera application and took a few shots of the beasts. Star sat up in the passenger seat of the car and watched the beasts as well. "Aren't they gorgeous?" he asked her.

BOOM!

The shot stunned Dannie and Star. They sank down in their seats, hoping they were not the intended marks. Seconds later, Dannie heard a shrieking howl. He was too scared to peek his head back up, so he stayed crouched down with Star. A thick quilt concealed them from any passing eyes but attracted so much heat from the sun. Dannie felt like he was sitting in a sauna and could not take the heat any longer. He pulled the quilt from over his face, risking exposure.

"Damn Dale, you actually hit it," a voice yelled out.

Dannie sat up and peeked from behind one of the headrests. The group flooded out the two homes and approached the beasts, which were leaning against an SUV. As the group approached, the beasts howled but did not move. They had their guns drawn, but two of the men were carrying large control poles. Dannie could not get a good view of what was going on. Reaching down towards his lap, he patted the floor under him. His fingers landed on a hard rectangular object. He raised it and activated the video feature on the iPhone. Using the zoom feature, he would see a small trail of blood coming from the beasts. He stayed hidden in the car and used his phone as his eyes. As in the past, the new American History would be nothing but stories of violence and chaos.

CHAPTER 16

GEORGE POINTED HIS SHOTGUN at the beasts. He was ready to let off another shot if necessary. Blood trickled from the larger beast's leg, which amused the gunman. The slug ate through the flesh, leaving a massive wound that left the beast unable to stand on all fours properly. Still hunched over from the blast, the beast appeared to be acquiescent.

"Hurry up and get these ugly monsters. You know they are strong," Dale said. "Rob you're gon' get that little one and Benny you got the mom."

Rob and Benny were the largest men in the group and the obvious choice as the handlers for the beasts. Rob was short but had a very athletic build. Benny was chunky and as a former college football lineman, had the strength of three men. The men slowly approached, the tension in Rob's back traveled down to his feet as he inched forward. The smaller beast instinctively jumped in front of its wounded companion and growled at the approaching men. WHACK! The force of the control pole, driven against the top of its head knocked the beast to the hot concrete. Benny pulled it back for another swing. WHACK! The beast hit the ground hard. The larger beast let out a roar that rattled the windows of every home on the block. BANG! BANG! Two shots from a Hi-Point handgun tore through the beast's previous wound. The beast dropped to the ground and whimpered in pain.

"Nice shot, Dana." Dale complimented the thin woman as she readjusted her hands around the bulky weapon.

"Just doing my job boss," she replied proudly.

Stepping over the smaller fallen body, Dale stared at the hairy beast and smiled as he pressed the barrel of his rifle against the top of its head. "When it comes to the battle between man and beast, man will always win. We have seen how powerful these creatures can be and now we witness how powerful we can be. Our former government created these monsters, and our new government will ensure we slaughter each and every one of them. You all will go down in history as pioneers, as warriors and as saviors of the human race." Dale reached into one of the pockets of his camo cargo pants and pulled out one of the gas canisters. "We have witnessed the effects of this weapon, courtesy of that weak government and together we will find a cure for the terrible disease that turned some of our loved ones into these," he announced, digging his rifle deeper into the beast's head. "Rob, take this piece of shit over there, and string it up," he ordered, pointing to one of the houses.

Rob pulled the wire of the control pole, constricting it around the beast's neck. It began to squirm out of control, almost causing Rob to lose his grip. He gave the wire another tug, which left the beast no other option but to save its energy and focus solely on breathing. It panted uncontrollably as Rob drug it down the street, up the steps and into the house. Dana and one other member of the group assisted him. Her finger danced around the trigger as she begged the beast to give her a reason to put every bullet she had left into its skull.

"Damn can I get a little help?" Rob asked as he struggled to drag the hundred and twenty-pound beast up the steps. Lifting that much weight at the gym was nothing, but it was much heavier at the end of a six-foot pole.

"There is no way in hell I'm putting my gun away to help you," Dana replied.

"Me either," Sam agreed. "The first chance that monster gets, it will kill all three of us and I ain't dying today."

"I'm going to kill you if you don't help me get this thing upstairs," Rob barked.

Dana chuckled as she watched the two man square off face to face. She knew all about Rob's temper and knew he would rip the rifle out of Sam's hand and beat him to death with it. *Typical man shit*, she thought, realizing neither man was backing down. "Let me go tell Dale we need some help since you two idiots want to play around. I'm sure he would appreciate your hard work," she threatened knowing just how to get the men to back down.

"How 'bout you get Dale's dick out your mouth," Rob said knowing the consequences would be deadly if Dale had to be summoned. Both men grabbed the pole and worked their way up the flight of stairs and into one of the bedrooms. A metal chain dangled from a post in the closet, which had been prepared in advance. The men loosened the control pole wire from around the beast's neck and replaced it with the thick chain.

"Be a good girl and keep an eye on your twin," Rob said as he walked by Dana and smacked her ass.

BANG! BANG!

Dana's finger slammed back on the trigger, as another bullet released from the gun. This time her target was not the beast, she had aimed at Rob.

"If you ever fuckin' touch me again, the next ones won't be at that wall."

Rob smirked, knowing just how to get under her skin. He knew two things pissed Dana off, questioning her loyalty to Dale and disrespecting her in any way. He cut his eye over at the two precise shots that were just inches from his head. *That bitch is crazy.*

"I know you motherfuckers didn't shoot that damn creature," Dale shouted, watching Rob and Sam exit the home. He stood on the step across the street as the other members of the group struggled to pull the three hundred pound beast up the steps.

"Hell no, your little girlfriend tried to shoot me," Rob responded.

Dale laughed because he knew how defensive Dana got when someone tested her. She could easily hold her own, and that is exactly what attracted him to her. He grabbed the control pole from Rob and wrapped it around the neck of the large beast. Now with two poles and all six men pulling, they were able to get the beast into the house. Dale looked at the beast that appeared to be submissive to his will. He could almost see its human traits resurfacing because an animal its size would have fought until the end. The group spent months hunting and studying the beasts. During the studies, they observed some of the beasts display superhuman strength, as well as each one become submissive once it was injured. It was during those studies when they learned what the beasts' weakness was. They were not sure what caused that reaction, but he was definitely using it to his advantage. Dale's job was to conduct a field study and bring back more specimens for more advanced testing. That was the only thing keeping the two beasts alive. Dale delivered a strong thrust kick, which sent the beast rolling down the basement stairs. Four members of the group chained it up in the basement as they were ordered.

CHAPTER 17

KYLE RAN DOWN THE stairs, stumbling on the last few steps and luckily regaining his balance. He hoped his eyes didn't see what he thought they did. He made his way by the stewing vomit on the kitchen floor and stuck his head out the window. He had yet to speak a word and only spent seconds in the window before pulling his head back and turning to the others. "Yo man what the hell is going on?" Marcus asked, wondering while Kyle suddenly became so jittery. He was used to the cool and calm Kyle that could stare in the face of death and not blink.

Kyle didn't say a word; he just walked out the kitchen door and onto a raised deck. *Who the hell would do this?* He looked over the ledge and never said a word to the others. Marcus and Candice had to see what Kyle was so worked up about and once they did, they couldn't stomach the sight. Marcus would have vomited some more, but there was nothing left in his body. Candice hastily ran back inside the house in disbelief to what her eyes just saw.

"What kind of monsters would do this?" Marcus knew he wouldn't get an answer. Deep down he knew he wasn't referring to the kind of monsters that had claws and razor-sharp fangs. These kind of monsters were human and so prosaic you wouldn't recognize them for what they truly are until it is entirely too late. Both men stood silently, as their eyes wandered back and forth between the three piles or deceased beasts that filled the alleyway. There had to be over fifty hairy bodies piled on top of each other, rotting away. The smell was ten times worse than the basement and much more potent.

Both men stood on the porch and stared at the numerous bodies that coated the alleyway. Someone had slaughtered beast after beast and left them all in heaps, to decay in the summer heat. It was a complete massacre. Kyle shined his light over the bodies and saw the bullet holes that riddled their hairy flesh. Over fifty bodies and not one appeared to be moving. Some of them still had clothing on and were significantly different in appearance from most. They were more similar to Chloe, right before Kyle put her out of her misery. He dropped his head, thinking about his baby girl and everything she had been through during her last days.

"Umm guys." Candice's shaky voice sounded from behind them. Kyle figured she was there to summons them back into the house and away from the man-made cemetery in the back alley. They slowly turned, only to find her standing at the door in tears. A Colt King Cobra was forced against her temple, as the gunman had his arm wrapped around her neck.

"Let her go," Kyle ordered, raising his gun at the mystery gunman.

"Yall better drop your weapons or this bitch is gon' get it," Sam replied. His hand clenched the revolver as his finger danced around the trigger.

"You don't have to do this man. You can take whatever you want, just let her go," Marcus suggested.

"I want your fuckin' guns asshole. Now drop them on the floor and kick them over to me."

Both men raised their arms, and slowly lowered their firearms to the floor. Neither wanted any harm to come to Candice, so cooperating was their best bet. Marcus was the first to drop his gun and immediately kicked it over to the gunman that was holding his girlfriend hostage. Sam's eyes followed the pistol as it slid in his direction. *BOOM! BOOM!* The eyes that followed the pistol had now rolled to the back of Sam's head as he fell backward. The force of the two headshots sent chunks of brain tissue flying out the back of his head. Sam's lifeless body hadn't hit the ground yet before shots were being fired from inside the house. The trio had no other choice but to crouch down under the window to take cover. Kyle was the closest to the door and blindly returned fire. Marcus and Candice were showered with glass as bullets ripped through the kitchen window. Marcus brushed pieces of shattered glass from his clothing and took advantage of the opportunity that presented itself. He stuck his hand up and fired aimlessly into the kitchen.

Shots were ringing out, bullets were whizzing by, and Candice was stuck between two men that could desperately use her help. Her selfish decision not to carry a gun had backfired. The knife she usually possessed was useless in this situation. She covered her ears and looked at Sam's body, remembering the vow she made never to be a victim again. A vow that was broken once he stepped foot into the home and saw her standing in the kitchen holding a knife. She wished she could grab her knife and drive it right into his chest. Candice's eyes lit up as she cast an eye over Sam's body. The Colt revolver was still in his hand. She quickly grabbed the gun and joined Marcus in the kitchen window, placing six shots into the living room.

The additional gunfire was enough to allow Kyle to slip into the kitchen. Once he did, he spotted one of their attackers wounded against the stove. Two to the chest put him down quick, as Kyle continued advancing. The sudden cease-fire let him know that either the group was out of rounds or they were reloading. He figured his two partners were out of ammunition but didn't know they had entered the home behind him and grabbed the gun off the deceased. Kyle had an angle on the living room and was left unexposed. Marcus stood next to Candice, who was in possession of a pistol they just picked up and had it aimed at the basement. Anyone who emerged from the basement would find themselves on the other end of some hot rounds. The sound of footsteps descending the stairs made Kyle salivate. Sweat covered his brow as he performed a mag-save reload and took aim on the step. Using his sharpshooter aim, he fired as soon as he saw legs. The woman coming down the stairs stood no chance as bullets ripped through her lower body, causing her to tumble down the remaining steps.

"Agh," she yelled as she hit the floor. She had a clear view of Marcus and pulled the trigger, with her gun pointed at his head. CLICK. She ran upstairs to reclaim the ammunition the group left behind but failed to realize her pistol magazine was empty. Kyle had left the duffel bag he filled upstairs, and she came down with it. She rummaged through the bag, snagging rounds that matched her gun. The woman dropped the magazine of the useless weapon and attempted to crawl and reload, as blood flooded from her leg wounds. Her jaws clenched as pain seared through her body. The pain was nothing compared to the burning sensation she felt in her shoulder as two bullets ripped through her skin. "Agh shit," she yelled out, dropping the gun and rounds as she fell back. She could do nothing but lay still on the floor and stare at the ceiling, hoping the next shot would send her to her maker.

"Don't shoot," a voice yelled out from the living room.

Kyle knew it was only a matter of time before this would happen and glad it wasn't his lips that had to speak those words. He dropped the magazine from his rifle and checked the remaining rounds. *That's at least twelve rounds.* He reinserted the magazine and yelled out, "Show yourself." Kyle looked at Marcus, pointed two fingers at his eyes and then one at the basement door.

"I got it," Marcus said as he readjusted his aim from the target he sent two shots through, back to the basement door. In the back of his mind, he knew that someone coming up would have had the drop on them for a brief second. He left himself a mental note because it was not a mistake he wanted to make again.

"Show yourself, and you better have your fuckin' hands up," Kyle order as he slowly surfaced from his point of cover. His aim was locked in on a young man who was shaking like a tambourine. He could not have been older than twenty-one and was frail too.

"Please don't kill me," the boy begged.

"Who the fuck are you and why are you here?" Kyle asked as he stuck his rifle in the boy's face.

"Ummm, Ummm," the boy stuttered.

"Don't tell him shit," cough, cough. A violent cough coming from the woman's mouth contained a mixture of saliva and blood. "If you say anything Dale is going to rip your little head off dumbass."

"Dale? Who is Dale?" Kyle asked the boy before being interrupted again by the wounded woman.

"Dale is the devil, and he should be coming in here at any second to kill your ass."

TAT! TAT! TAT! TAT! TAT! TAT! TAT!

Kyle recognized the unique sound of an AK-47 being fired and immediately dove on the ground. Thinking help had arrived the boy ran towards the front door, which was slightly ajar. From the prone position, Kyle sent a single shot through the boy's right calf, dropping him immediately. The gunfire outside continued and was accompanied by coughing and loud laughter from the woman. "Oh you assholes are about to get it," she said while laughing, knowing the other members of her group were right outside.

The sound of tires screeching off seemed to silence the war outside. Kyle looked around; noticing the chaos they created inside the house had not been added to. AK rounds would have surely ripped through the house like paper, but they didn't. Something didn't sit right with Kyle, and he wanted answers. "Listen, you are going to tell me everything I need to know or you are going to end up like your friends." The boy looked around at the three bodies that were not moving, including the arrogant woman who was no longer laughing or coughing. Tears began to fall from his eyes as he began to speak.

"Ok, my name is Kenny and when all this shit went down with the government and stuff, I was recruited by my best friend's dad. Mr. Benny had found a bunch of people that hated what the government did to us and planned to take over the little that was left behind. The group is called THE ASSOCIATION and is ran by some scary dude name Micah. I think Micah started The Association, but he has a bunch of guys by his side. One of those guys is Dale, and he is our leader. Dale is the one that brought us here a week ago."

"So you are the monsters that slaughtered those beasts out back."

The boy hung his head down in shame. "Yes, yes we did. It was part of some experiment Dale was in charge of. See the gas that the military was dropping changes people into those monsters. We found that out through the tests. If you breathe in the gas, it will kill you and then change you into one of those creatures. We also found out that the creatures are attracted to the gas. We dropped some canisters in the back of the house and watched as those creatures showed up by the dozens."

"So what was the point in killing them?"

"Because Dale wants them all dead. He wants the human race to be superior, and we don't want those things around."

"So if your job was to kill those things, why did you come back?"

"We don't kill them all. Some of them we take alive for testing. We were coming back for the two beasts we chained up."

"Two? There's only one down there."

"Yeah, the other one is across the street."

Kyle hopped up and grabbed the boy by his collar. If the group had also secured a house across the street, that would explain why the gunfire stopped. They could be conducting surveillance and planning another attack on the group. If they were, Kyle didn't plan on sticking around to find out. He had Marcus tie the boy up in the basement while he gathered the weapons from the deceased. They were now carrying around three bags full of ammunition and weaponry but were running low on food and supplies. Kyle knew they had a long journey ahead of them.

C.L. LOWRY

CHAPTER 18

"**What the FUCK you** mean you were ambushed?" Micah asked. His voice sounded more like a roar of a lion inside the large room.

"Listen, all I know is we went back to get those creatures we tied up and once we pulled up, we started getting shot at."

"By who?"

"I don't know. I don't even know where it came from. Bodies just started dropping, and we got out of there. Me, Rob and Benny."

"I sent you out on that mission with seven other people. You're tellin' me that you couldn't battle it out?"

"We did battle it out, but some people split up, and we were outnumbered."

"Outnumbered? Since all this shit started, we haven't run into a group larger than five. So how the hell was a group of more than ten able to form without us knowing?"

Dale made very little eye contact with Micah, knowing he wasn't being truthful about the events that took place. His pride wouldn't allow him to admit he made a mistake and left his group stranded once things got a little hot. He didn't return one shot or give any orders for his people to take cover. The only thing he did was worry about himself and his two henchmen, leaving the others to fend for themselves. "Listen all I know is that somebody was waiting for us when we got back there. Those creatures might still be in the houses. Give me twenty able-body men and women and let me go back to retrieve the creatures and anyone that may have survived."

"Twenty more people Dale? How many more lives do you want to lose? Since we formed The Association, there have been fifty of our people that have gone out into this new world and have not returned. Fifty-seven now since you came bearing this bad news. We are losing more people than we are gaining."

"But we have close to a thousand people here —"

"— and we need to continue growing. We need to build up The Association, so we are the most powerful force in the country. This will be our land. Since the moment we took you in, your job was to recruit people and convince them to join us. It has been three months since the chaos, and I have yet to see you bring anyone in; you just come back telling me how many lives we are losing. I know there are other groups that have formed and will form, so you need to let me know if you are an asset to The Association or a liability."

"I'm definitely an asset, and you know that."

Micah reached on the table and grabbed a fifty caliber Desert Eagle. He raised the gun and pointed it directly between Dale's eyes. "This is your last chance so if you fuck this up, don't bother coming back."

Dale was never one to back down or be intimidated, but he saw how Micah's finger slid around the trigger. He also saw the small group of men standing behind Micah, waiting to finish what he started. Although Dale had a powerful position within The Association, he was now being humiliated in front his peers and Micah would eventually have to pay for the blatant disrespect he displayed. *I'm going to slit your fuckin' throat,* he thought as he looked into the eyes of his leader. "I won't let you down sir," Dale muttered, knowing he would have rather said what was on his mind.

"Ok, so this is what's going to happen. I am not giving you twenty men. Shit, I'm not even giving you ten. You, Benny and Rob are going to go back to that block you ran from and you are going to bring back my beasts, my guns and the vehicles you took. If you don't, I will personally put a bullet in all of your heads." Micah extended his arm and used his pistol to forcefully nudged Dale's head back. "Now get the fuck out of here." Micah didn't know it, but he signed his own death certificate. Dale was not a man to be underestimated. Unlike Micah, Dale knew there were small pockets within the city where groups were forming and they wreaked havoc on those groups. They raped, tortured and murdered all in the name of The Association. So regardless of the outcome, The

Association would have to deal with those consequences one day.

Dale walked out the room, slamming the door behind him. He walked down the stairs of the old high school, which had been converted into the headquarters for The Association. Benny and Rob were waiting for him in the Mercury, hoping he would come out with good news.

"So are we going back there?" Benny asked eagerly as Dale approached.

Dale looked around at the members of the organization. Each group served a purpose, whether it was harvesting food, collecting supplies, assisting the few doctors that joined the group or experimenting with the animals. In his opinion, there was no need to expand. *The more people, the more problems*, he thought. Little did he know, he would eventually become a problem himself. Dale knew what his assignments were, but he didn't feel the need to bring more people into the group for nothing. A spot in The Association had to be earned, in his eyes. Unfortunately, Micah was willing to give out free memberships to the most ruthless organization of the new world, just to expand. Dale wanted that top spot, and he planned to take it.

"Yo man, are we going back or not?"

"Yeah, but we're out," Dale replied as he entered the vehicle.

"Out, what you mean we're out?" Rob inquired.

"That motherfucker Micah, said he wants us to go back to get his guns, the trucks, and those fuckin' creatures. He said if we do not deliver, he is going to kill us. I told yall about him since the beginning. I knew this would happen."

Benny slammed his fists on the vehicle's dashboard. "We don't answer to him. We work for Adina, and she knew what the plans were from the beginning."

"Man, who the fuck you think she's gon' stand by? Us or her man?"

"I'm sure she won't just let him kick us out of the organization we helped build," Rob said. "Our families are here. What will happen to them?" He could not imagine the possibility of experiencing the type of pain they had inflicted on many innocent families. Killing the fathers in front of their young children, raping mothers and daughters, and releasing the chemical gas into houses just to watch a family suffer through the painful transformation into beasts. The men did some of the most unthinkable acts one could imagine and would now have to face the same fate as the innocent families they tortured.

"For the sake of our families, let's just go back and get the things," Benny suggested, thinking about what would happen to his wife and son if they were never to return.

Dale wasted no time once he heard his crew's statements. He sped off down the street and exited through the large barrier that separated The Association from the ruins of Philadelphia. Formerly known as Cottman Avenue, the road they traveled was once the main vein through the middle-class neighborhood of Northeast Philadelphia. Immediately outside the area claimed by The Association, homes and businesses were intentionally burned to the ground. There was not much infrastructure for miles, which was Adina's idea. She had members of their organization torch buildings, some with families still inside. She wanted a clear vantage point to see anyone or anything that approached their new civilization. The buildings served no purpose to her. She would stand on the roof of their headquarters and watch as large flames devoured portions of her city. Nevertheless, Micah let his queen rule with an iron fist, even though their visions for the new world were so different from his. Micah was more interested in rebuilding for the people and finding a cure to reverse the effects of the chemical gas, while Adina was more so interested in rebuilding for herself and ruling through fear.

CHAPTER 19

"**Watch your step**," Kyle said, being careful not to step on any of the beasts that were sprawled out throughout the alleyway. Now that the sun had risen, it was clear to see the carnage Dale's group had caused. There were furry bodies and blood everywhere, and the sight of it all was churning Marcus' stomach. He had vomited a few more times as the group navigated through the mess. "Keep your eyes open; there's no telling who or what is out here." Marcus and Candice moved much more tactically than they had when they first met Kyle. After being snatched up in the house, Candice knew how important awareness was no matter how safe or secure the environment seemed to be. Her steak knives sat in her backpack, and she had become very familiar with her newly acquired revolver. Luckily, they were able to reload all of their weapons with the ammunition they attained when they first entered the house. There were so many bodies; it was almost impossible for the group to walk side by side. There was only enough room for them to stack up with Kyle leading and Marcus holding up the rear. The lack of sleep and nutrition was beginning to catch up to them all. The bags they carried felt as if they weighed a hundred pounds each, which was a weight they wouldn't last long with. The bags were filled with necessities, so ditching some items to lighten the load was not an option.

"Agh." The group was almost to the corner when Marcus yelled out. Kyle turned and saw a paw on Marcus' shoulder. The claws were digging deep into his skin. Kyle quickly took out his knife and stabbed the beast in the wrist, causing it to loosen its grip. Next was an elbow strike, downward onto its forearm, which immediately snapped. The crack was like stepping on a tree branch. The beast's broken arm dangled as Marcus maneuvered away from its reach. He raised his gun and decided to take the beast's life.

"No," Kyle yelled, placing his hand on top of Marcus' gun and forcing him to lower it. "Let it be." A sense of compassion was beginning to weigh heavily on Kyle. Although they had transformed into what some may describe as monsters, Kyle knew deep down inside there had to be some existence of the human they once were. Seeing as though he had to take the life of his own child after she mutated, he knew firsthand the pain and guilt he still felt for pulling the trigger. Marcus watched as the beast continued reaching out towards him. It was injured and stuck in one of the body piles, so he wasn't concerned with it becoming free. Its gurgling sounds were hardly intimidating, which was very different from the devilish howl the group has witnessed one of the beasts make. Marcus was still confused as to why Kyle didn't let him take the shot.

"Let me see it," Candice said, pulling his shirt collar to the side and revealing the fresh wounds on his shoulder. "It doesn't look that bad; you're lucky baby."

"We can patch it up later; I'll be alright." Between the blood seepage from the wounds on his back and now the fresh wound, Marcus' shirt looked like a butcher's apron after a long day of work.

"Stay close," Kyle said as they approached the corner of the alleyway. He knew they were going to be exposed as they worked their way across the street. Peeking from behind the corner, he noticed the streets were quiet. "We got to make a run for it."

"Where are we running to?" Candice asked.

"To the alleyway across the street. We will get into the house through the back door."

"But what if someone is at the back door?"

"Well, that's a risk we just have to take unless you rather go ring the doorbell."

"Alright chill out," Marcus butted in, not appreciating the sarcasm that was being thrown at his woman.

Kyle looked at the two, as they returned annoyed stares. He took off running; his boots kicked up dust as they slammed on the hot concrete. With his rifle aimed, Kyle cleared the block as he ran by and quickly hit the corner of the alleyway. His brown eyes searched the alleyway as he located numerous dead bodies that cluttered the alley. Remaining statue-still, he hugged the wall as Marcus and Candice crept around the corner. They clearly mimicked amateur tactical moves they probably saw on the television show COPS, which amused Kyle.

"Bang, bang," he whispered, letting his companions know they would be dead if he happened to be the enemy.

"What the fuck was that about? You just gon' leave us back there like that?" Marcus said. He wasn't in the mood for the little games Kyle wanted to play. A part of him wanted to back down, but he was still upset at the way Kyle had spoken to Candice.

Kyle looked Marcus up and down, not threatened by his towering height and larger frame. *Make one fuckin' move and I'm going to gut you like a fish*, Kyle thought. His hand slowly gripped the knife on his waistband. He waited for Marcus to raise his gun or throw a punch. It would be a quick, yet painful death for the battered man.

Candice said nothing. Instead, she stood between the two men, which made it impossible for either of them to strike without hitting her. Marcus looked down at Candice's displeased face and immediately rolled his eyes. Clutching all of his anger into his right fist, Marcus took several deep breaths to calm himself down. He knew her all too well, and the look she was giving him was her way of telling him that he was wrong. Although she appreciated her man sticking up for her, she couldn't ignore the fact that the only reason they both were alive was because of Kyle. "Listen, we all need to stick together. Stop this nonsense," she told both men.

"It ain't me; it's him. He's the one that just tried to leave us back there," Marcus replied.

Kyle laughed at the response. "Listen tough guy, since you're so big and bad, you can lead the way from now on."

"That shit don't phase me. You think I'm scared or something?"

Kyle didn't say another word. He simply stepped behind them both and began guarding the rear. Since he assumed Marcus' responsibility, Marcus had no choice but to work his way to the house. During their little spat, Marcus never noticed the bodies in the alleyway. It was one thing walking through piles of the creatures, but it was another stepping over human corpses. *What the fuck*, he thought as his eyes wandered around the entire alley. The group was walking past vacant homes that could have contained surprises, their heads needed to be on a constant rotation. The beating sun slowly drained their energy, causing them to crave a cool beverage. The dryness in the back of their throats needed to be moistened.

Stepping forward, it was obvious the number of dead bodies began to increase as they advanced further into the alley. The summer heat was blasting on each corpse, which allowed for the particular scent of decomposition to float in the air. Marcus' stomach flipped with each breath he inhaled. He wanted to put on his gas mask, but his pride would not allow him to display any form of weakness in Kyle's presence.

"Right here." Kyle noticed the abundance of shell casings surrounding a pile of bodies and figured it was worth a shot to check the house. He stood on the corner of the wall and looked at Marcus, waiting for him to continue the lead.

"What if it's a trap?" Marcus asked. The sudden change in his demeanor and tone told Kyle everything he wanted to know. Fear was written all over his face, but he had already made his bed. Once he saw the smirk on Kyle's face, he moved toward the rear door and checked the knob. A part of him wanted the door to be locked, and the other part of him wished Kyle was still in front. Leading a group of people into the unknown is not for the weak and Marcus was finding that out the hard way. He twisted the knob, and he felt a knot drop into his stomach. The door began slowly creeping open.

CHAPTER 20

The Playing Card Flipped through his fingers before Micah flicked it onto the table. The card landed face up on a stack of papers, revealing the Ace of Spades. "Where are we at with a cure for this disease?" he asked the group of five that sat across from him at the table.

"Well sir, we were able to successfully duplicate the chemical gas which has been tested and proven to cause the same effects as the gas used by the military. Unfortunately, every antidote we have engineered seems not to be effective in reversing the negative effects of the gas."

"Well, when can I expect it to be effective?" Micah asked, leaning forward on the table and looking at each of them directly.

"We— Well, we can't say for sure at this very moment. We need more time."

Micah removed the chrome pistol from his waistband and placed it on the table, with the barrel facing the five researchers. They all began squirming in their seats, trying their best not to be Micah's targets. He slammed his fists on the table and then swiped at the stack of papers, sending them flying across the room. This was not the first time Micah's temper reared its ugly head. Although he had intentions to find a cure that could turn the beasts back into humans, he did not plan to just dispense it out of good will. He had plans to sell it to the highest bidder. After seeing the effects the chemical gas had on American citizens, Micah believed there would be countries lined up to get their hands on the duplicate of the chemical weapon as well as the antidote. That could mean billions for him along with the resources to rebuild the country under his reign.

"I told yall I wanted a cure by this week and yall have not met the deadline. You need to tell me what the holdup is."

"We just need more time and samples to test. We haven't had a new creature brought to the facility in weeks. The ones that are currently in the pit are under observation."

"Listen, the only reason you five are still alive is because of the work you do for me. If you cannot deliver the work I have requested, I guarantee you that I will personally rip each of your hearts out myself and feed them to the creatures in the pit."

"That won't be necessary. We will deliver results," one of the researchers claimed. "Once we get new specimens, we can begin. We also need to conduct field studies, so we can observe the creatures interact with each other in their own environment."

"How about I send some of my people to Area X. What would you need them to do?"

"We need them to perform tests. Since your last group saw the large amount of creatures in that area, I think it's safe to say that those things made that area their home. We need to know why so many of them are flocking together and what is attracting them to that specific location. We want to know how the creatures react to the gas and how they are surviving. So if a team can go out and secure a building for us to operate out of, that would be very helpful."

Micah remained silent. He thought about the request made by his researchers and the resources needed to complete such a mission. Sending a small team out wouldn't be the hardest part of the mission, but the researchers only saw one side of the equation. Micah knew he would need to staff the building with security and send them with supplies. He didn't want to risk his team being compromised and someone getting a hold of his plans. The tapping of his fingers on the table produced a steady rhythm. The researchers looked on as the gears in Micah's head began churning. The tapping increased and was now accompanied by the tapping of his foot on the worn, wooden floor panels. Each of the researchers flinched when the tapping turned into a closed fist slamming on the table.

"I'm going to send an initial team out to survey the area. If it has the potential for occupancy, we will send a larger group out with one of you and the field studies can be completed."

"Yes, sir. Thank you."

"Now get the fuck back to work."

CHAPTER 21

CAUTIOUSLY STEPPING INSIDE THE home, pieces of shattered glass cracked beneath their feet. It seemed the more they attempted to tiptoe into the basement, the louder the cracks became. The natural sunlight assisted them as they maneuvered through the dark, eerie home. Candice jumped back once something emerged from the shadows, which hugged the corners of the basement. Placing her hand over her chest, she somehow tried to slow down her rapid heartbeat after realizing it was just a stray cat venturing through the door the group opened as they entered. The layout of the basement was very similar to that of the house across the street, reminding the group of the sick individuals they had gone up against. Taking a huge gulp, Marcus began to ascend the stairs. If the layout served them right, they would end up in the kitchen of this home as well. Once again, he was faced with a closed door. He slowly reached out, but his sweaty palm slid off the knob. Kyle was disgusted in the way Marcus carried himself. Such a large man had so much fear in his heart. *Sooner or later, that fear is going to cost him his life.*

As soon as the door opened, Marcus stared at the dirty red mark on the kitchen floor. The horrible stain was the sign the group needed, confirming they had entered the right home. Using his pathetic television tactics, Marcus cut the tight corner and cleared a path into the living room. Kyle passed through the kitchen, immediately noticing it had been ransacked. The hunger pangs were getting worse, and their food supply was low. They had enough food to last two weeks at best, and that is only if they stretched it.

"Look at this," Candice said as her fingers spread apart two window blinds, giving her a clear view of the street.

Kyle worked his way over to the same window. He saw the holes that decorated the U-Haul trucks and noticed the bodies that were on the ground, near the trucks.

THUMP! THUMP!

The noise coming from the second floor of the home grabbed everyone's attention. Kyle wasted no time working his way up the stairs, looking to eliminate any threats that came his way. He cleared the hallway and moved straight to the front bedroom, while Candice searched the middle room and Marcus headed to the back. Kyle's eyes lit up when he entered the front bedroom. A pile of canned goods and bags of potato chips sat on a table near the window. Safety was not a concern to the soldier that was usually vigilant whenever he entered an unknown area; he never searched the room and focused only on the food. Walking over a cluster of spent AK rounds, Kyle grabbed a bag of the chips and ripped it open. The stale chips made his mouth water and satisfied him as if it were a steak dinner from Morton's Steakhouse.

Marcus pushed open the bedroom door and was immediately overwhelmed by a familiar stench. He heard a small growl and knew exactly what was in the room. Seeing no need to investigate further, he closed the door and turned to see Candice eyeing him up in the hallway.

"What's wrong?" she asked.

"Nothing."

Candice caught a whiff of the rancid odor that arose when Marcus opened the bedroom door. "What the hell is that smell?"

"One of those creatures is in there."

"Yo come here," Kyle yelled, looking at the two conversing in the hallway.

He threw them two bags of chips, once they stepped foot into the room. The group looked like a pack of hyenas devouring their prey. It had been so long since they tasted the salty snack and enjoyed each bite, despite the extra effort required to chew through the stale chips. The room was silent for about ten minutes as they finished the chips and treated themselves to packets of instant oatmeal that accompanied the snacks they shared.

"That was so good," Candice said, licking the salt off her fingertips.

"It's about time we lucked up. I was going crazy without eating," Marcus mumbled with a mouth full of oatmeal.

"Kyle, pass me another —"

Door slam.

They all jumped up with weapons in hand. "Get in the corner," Kyle suggested as he took up a crouching position in the deep left corner of the room. His rifle was pointed at the doorway, ready to take out anybody that stepped foot into his target zone. Candice stood in the closet, and Marcus was hunched down behind an armoire. Footsteps could be heard coming up the stairs and into the hallway.

"Oh, what the fuck. Who ate our shit?"

Noticing the empty potato chips bags on the floor, the man walked into the room and picked one of the bags off the floor. He also noticed the open packets of oatmeal that were left on the ground. He kneeled down and picked up one of the oatmeal packets. There was fresh blood on the packet and more on the tan carpet that covered the floor. Cutting his eye, he spotted a trail of the blood on the carpet. The trail led to the armoire and that is exactly where the guy aimed, standing to his feet and presenting his weapon.

"I wouldn't do that if I were you," Kyle said softly, causing the male to look back in his direction. Staring at Kyle was enough of a distraction to allow Marcus to emerge from behind the armoire and place his gun on the man's cheek. Candice also revealed herself, with her revolver pointed at the stranger's chest. Without being asked to do so, he dropped his weapon and raised his hands.

"Well, would you look at this. I thought you all were dead," the man stated. The comment confused the group because they never met the man before.

"Who are you?" Kyle asked.

"The name's Daniel, I prefer Danielle, but you can just call me Dannie," he replied. "This little beauty queen is my best friend, Star." The brown Yorkshire Terrier greeted the group with a soft bark. "She's a little shy, so don't mind her."

"So Daniel —"

"DANNIE."

"— Dannie, why did you say you thought we were dead?"

"Because I saw when you got to the house. I knew you weren't part of that other crew because the way you moved was more so avoiding trouble, rather than inviting it. Those other guys were all about trouble. When I saw them come back to the house and heard all the gunfire going on, I was sure they went in there and slaughtered yall. But it seems the angels were watching over you three last night."

Kyle looked at the AK-47 Dannie dropped on the floor. "So that was you that dropped the rest of those assholes outside?"

"You are correct handsome," Dannie said while taking a bow as if he were starring in a Broadway play. He could smell the roses that would be thrown on the stage and hear the applause from the crowd. The group watched as Dannie put on an imaginary show, waving to the audience that was actually the closet door.

"Why?" Candice said, interrupting the dancing man.

"Why what?"

"Why did you help us?"

Dannie threw his arms in the air and struck a pose, which was both dramatic and amusing to Candice. "Well girlfriend, let me tell you. I am just a kind-hearted individual, and I felt it was my American duty to protect you from those evil people that would have butchered you. I guess some would say I'm a hero, but I don't want you to think that. To you, I'm just lil' Dannie and this is Queen Star, and we are your new best friends." He ended the statement by twirling around the room with Star in his arms. The small Yorkshire had her tongue dangling out her mouth as she enjoyed being embraced and spun around.

Kyle turned his head around and peeked out the window. "So Mr. Hero, you were saving us huh?"

"Yes, I was."

"Then tell me something. Why are the bodies on this side of the street and not over where we were?"

"Huh?" Dannie asked, stopping himself in mid-twirl.

"You heard me. The bodies are over here. Your lying ass wasn't saving us; you were saving yourself. They were coming to this house, not just the one we were in."

"Now that makes sense," Marcus added. "There's a creature tied up in that back room. So they were going to come in here to get it and once they found you, they would have fed you and your little dog to their pet beast."

A knot sat in the back of Dannie's throat as the truth began to reveal itself. The conclusion the group came to was correct. On that night, the members of The Association had split up and Dannie knew once he was spotted with their food and weapons, that there was no chance he would have made it out alive. Once he began dropping bodies, he watched three of the members of The Association get into a car and speed off. He fired shots at the fleeing vehicle but wasn't sure if he hit anyone. Once morning came and he didn't see any movement on the street, he scavenged the bodies for weapons and supplies. There was no way he was going to stick around for another wave of the militia to return to the block for revenge. He had no idea Kyle, Candice, and Marcus had slipped into the back of the home.

CHAPTER 22

The door slammed as they exited the vehicle. After what happened the last time they were on the block, certain precautions had to be taken. They hugged the front of the properties during their approach. All eyes were focused on the windows, ensuring no one would take aim on them without them being able to do so in return. It was a while before they reached their destination. It was a run down, turnkey home in the middle of the block. The rustic, mahogany front door was standing open and welcoming the three into the home. The wooden floor panels were scratched up and loose. Being careful where they stepped, they attempted to avoid any possible soft spots on the floor that would send them crashing into the basement.

"It ain't shit down here. Let's check upstairs."

The men worked their way up the steps and into the bedrooms. Once the door opened, the sight of the mangled corpse sent two of the three men running out the room. Death loomed in the air, as the setting sun provided very little light in the room. The torso of the body had been cleaned out like a turkey on Thanksgiving. The face had been chewed off like a piece of jerky. Something inside him knew the identity of the deceased, but he examined the bloody remains in search of something familiar. A mole or birthmark would help, but with the amount of blood and ripped flesh across the body, it would be very difficult to locate. Was it even worth looking? Was it even worth knowing?

Rage filled his eyes, seeing the body restrained to the bed. Rope was tied around the hands and feet. He wanted to walk over and remove the restraints, but it seems like he was wearing cement shoes. His feet would not move, and he was left speechless by the torturous arrangement that had been created in the room. Pools of tears began to fill his eyes as the rage quickly turned into sadness. There it was; a small heart tattoo on the ankle of the corpse. Dale's worst fear had been confirmed; he was staring at Dana's mutilated body. The cement shoes had been lifted, and he began stepping slowly towards his girlfriend's corpse. The smell of rotting flesh had very little effect on the man that was the cause of so much devastation in the new world. The way a seasoned trash man could bear the smell of the trash truck is the way the Reaper could bear death's aroma, even if it meant he just lost the love of his life. Benny and Rob had family back on the grounds of The Association, but the only person Dale had in his life was tied to a full-size bed and missing her organs.

He reached the foot of the bed and began loosening the restraints. The rattle of a chain caught his attention as he turned and saw a beast coming towards him. BANG! He watched as it dropped to the floor and its brain exited its head. BANG! BANG! BANG! BANG! BANG! BANG! Dale did not stop firing until his Kel-Tec locked back and the magazine had emptied. His finger still slammed on the trigger as he continued aiming for the beast's head. Although he had killed the beast that took his girlfriend's life, he now was on the search for the person responsible for tying her up. The Reaper wanted revenge.

"Dale, are you alright?" Rob asked, running into the room after hearing the melee of gunshots. The atrocious stench sent him soaring back out the room.

Rob and Benny stood outside the door and watched as Dale slowly untied Dana's corpse. He did not say a word to them, and frankly, he did not need to because they got the hint. Rob knew how much Dana meant to Dale and although he could care less that she was dead, he knew his friend would not take it well.

"Is he going to be ok?" Benny asked Rob.

"Would you be ok, if you lost your wife?"

Benny felt a sharp pain in his chest, just at the thought of something happening to his wife. He looked back at the room and just shook his head, trying to imagine what emotions Dale was currently feeling. Little did he know, Dale would no longer be the same man they expected to rebuild the world alongside.

"This is where they had to be," Rob told Benny. Looking at all the shell casings that covered the floor.

They got the drop on us from right here, and we didn't even know it.

"Who do you think it was?"

"I have no idea, but take your pick. Look at how many families we slaughtered. Any and everybody should want to kill us."

Those words stuck with Benny. He was tired. Tired of robbing, tired of torturing and tired of killing. He knew they couldn't even try to keep count of how many innocent citizens they murdered in cold blood, under Dale's orders. There was no coming back from that type of evil, and there is no way to shake off those type of demons. Those demons will lurk forever and will follow them to the gates of hell. They picked up the empty cans and looked through the empty shell casings, in search of anything to bring back to Micah.

Benny put his fist through the wall. "There's nothing fuckin' here. We are dead men."

"Listen I'm sure Micah will be understanding. I know Adina will spare our lives. We have done so much work for her, and there is no way she would let anything happen to us."

"Let's check the house across the street."

"What about him?"

Rob looked down the hallway and into the darkness that filled the back room. "What about him?" he asked Benny. The two men walked towards the back room, but neither felt the need to go inside the black hole. Two monsters were lurking inside, one was dead, and the other was out for blood. "Dale, come on, we are going across the street," Rob yelled out. The two men didn't even wait for a response before exiting. They knew Dale all too well and knew he was defeated. They were sent on a mission that was literally impossible. The only hope they had would be bringing back the beasts, and Dale just put a bunch of holes in one of them. They had nothing to return to Micah.

Rob and Benny were still on high alert, as they exited the home. Watching for shooters in the windows or beasts that could emerge from any opening of the homes, they had their guns aimed in every direction. Rob cringed at the sight of his comrades' rotting bodies baking in the sun. Plump flies hovered over the corpses and maggots crawled through every crevice. Benny put his hand on Rob's shoulder, leading him away from the horrific scene and over in the direction of the U-Haul trucks. They were filled with holes, and the tires had been slashed. It was a clear message about the feelings toward The Association. "Cover me," he told Benny as he unlatched the rear door. Benny's gun was pointed directly at the door, so if anyone or anything popped out, he would be ready to take action. The door was pushed open, only to reveal emptiness inside the truck. They also checked the second truck, which revealed the same findings.

"Where the hell is the Jeep?" Benny asked, remembering the vehicles the crew drove to the block that night.

Rob looked up and down the block, wondering if someone had moved it. There were several parked cars in the area, but their vehicle could not be located.

"Maybe someone survived all of this and took the Jeep to head back to the camp."

Benny scratched his head, knowing there was a possibility that scenario could be true. "I guess so, but don't you think we would have seen them when we went back or in passing? We took the same route back."

"Yeah, we did. But you never know, maybe they took another way."

"Well if they did that means they may have the guns and extra ammo," Benny suggested, knowing how desperately they needed those items.

The men did not spend too much time on the streets, as paranoia began to set in. They were so used to being predators; it was hard to see themselves as prey. Coping with the fact they left their comrades behind was also in the back of their minds as they made their way inside the other home, the group once occupied. A combination of a week old pile of trash, dirty diapers, expired steak and warm, spoiled milk is the only comparison to the stench that hit them when they stepped into the home. They attempted to keep their guards up for any possible attacks, but it was useless as their focus was solely on the bodies. Between the horrendous odor and their extreme guilt, it was difficult for the duo to navigate through the house.

"There's nothing here. No guns, no ammo, nothing." Rob knocked over a dresser in the master bedroom.

"Well, what the fuck are we going to do Rob? We have nothing. They aren't going to just accept our excuses without having to pay a penalty."

"We have to take the chance. I don't know if anyone told you yet, but there is nothing left Benny. No more American dream bullshit, just the survival of the fittest."

"Exactly, we need to survive and that won't happen if we go back to the camp."

"Trust me I have a plan," Rob replied. A sinister smirk spread across his face as the gears in his brain began spinning.

They quickly exited the corpse-filled home and headed back to the car. Benny couldn't help but to look over at the house and wonder if Dale was still inside. A part of him wanted to wrap his muscular arms around his friend and drag him out the house, but he knew that would be a difficult task. If Dale were weaponless, Benny would have taken the risk but seeing as though he was currently armed with a Walther P99, Benny knew as soon as he attempted to get close Dale would take the shot. As soon as the men turned the corner, they were face to face with three beasts. Two of the beasts were lingering around the Mercury, and the other was feasting on a fresh body in the middle of the street. The left rear passenger door of the Mercury was standing open, and an orange backpack was on the ground, five feet from the vehicle.

Benny let off two shots at the beast in the street but to no avail. The shots missed and drew the attention of all three creatures. One leaped forward and swiped at the men, striking Benny in the arm. Rob got off three shots, which struck the closest beast in the abdomen. He quickly focused his attention to the other beast near the vehicle and let off four shots before hearing the clicking of his empty Ruger as he continued pulling the trigger. BANG! BANG! Benny took the last of his shots, finishing off the wounded beast that struck him. The other two beasts quickly retreated, leaving behind a trail of blood from the meal they dragged along during their retreat. Rob quickly jumped into the driver's seat and started the Mercury. Benny hopped in the back seat and grabbed the orange backpack when he closed the door. Smoke from the tires filled the air as the two raced off in the clunky sedan.

"What about Dale?" Benny asked.

"What about him?"

"We can't just leave him behind. You know those things will be creeping around."

"That's his problem."

"Come on Rob; he's our friend. We can't just do this."

"You got two seconds to shut the fuck up about Dale before I kick you out this fuckin' car. Dale didn't come out the house Benny. He doesn't give a fuck about us. If he did, he would be in this car with us, going back to The Association."

"I'm just saying —"

"I don't give a fuck what you're saying right now. We are going back home to our families."

CHAPTER 23

 around the street corners like a bat out of hell. Kyle's hands gripped the steering wheel as he made each turn. Navigating through the ruins of what was once prominent landmarks and infrastructure. Dannie was in the front seat singing Beyoncé, while Candice and Marcus napped in the backseat. The journey left the couple drained, physically and emotionally. The group didn't have an immediate plan but wanted to get out of the area in case more enemies worked their way to the target homes. Despite all they had been through, Kyle never got used to the sight and smell of decaying flesh. He fought years as a Marine to protect the country from foreign threats, only to face the reality that America's greatest threat was itself. When you spend decades trying to defy nature's law and experimenting with different diseases, the current state of affairs was inevitable. There was no way we as humans would not have to deal with the repercussions of our ignorant actions. Navigating the streets in the Jeep, mounds of rubbish surrounding them, Kyle did his best to keep his eyes solely on the cluttered road. Just months prior, he drove on that exact road and observed all the beautiful scenery Philadelphia had to offer.

The local strip mall, like all other buildings, fell victim to looters and pyromaniacs. Each store was nothing more than an empty shell. Memories of shopping on the very strip with Jacqui and Chloe popped in his head as he drove by the commercial corpse. The large windows that once provided shoppers a look into the hottest retail wear and gear only provided a look into what had become of law and order. Small animals could be observed running in and out each of the buildings. BANG! BANG! Kyle slammed on the brakes as he heard two shots coming from a short distance ahead. The first thing he thought was that the crew was under attack.

"What was that?" Marcus asked, awoken from his slumber by the sudden halt of the vehicle.

Dannie rolled down his window and looked out. "It sounded like gunshots, but maybe it was noth—"

BANG! BANG! BANG!

Everyone in the Jeep began ducking down, attempting to locate the source of the gunshots. Kyle pulled behind another vehicle on the side of the road, portraying the Jeep as being parked and abandoned. "Look at that," Candice stated, pointing towards a large amount of orange smoke emerging from the courtyard of another strip mall. Kyle pulled out the parking spot and crept up, towards the mall. He wanted to know what was causing the smoke. More gunshots sounded off followed up by horrifying screams. The smoke became thicker and as Kyle pulled up, he observed three people running from the courtyard. The two women had quite the distance in front the heavyset male who was struggling to pick up the pace. Suddenly several beasts rounded the corner, from the courtyard, and chased the trio. There were at least eight beasts, and they were different sizes and types. The trio didn't stand a chance against the speed of the beasts, as the distance between both groups quickly closed. Two of the beasts leaped on the heavyset man who screamed for mercy once he felt their claws rip through his blubbery flesh. Another beast joined in on the attack, biting the man's arm and ripping it from the rest of his body. Marcus cringed at the gruesome sight and rolled his window down.

BANG! BANG! BANG! BANG!

Normally Marcus would be puking after seeing someone's limb being ripped from their body but instead, he hung out the window and fired shots at the beasts who continued giving chase. His shots were precise, striking one beast three times and another once. The women continued running, hoping to evade the same fate their partner suffered. "I'm out," Marcus yelled out, ducking his head back into the window and attempted to reload his gun. Kyle stopped the car and reached down to retrieve his rifle.

"Keep driving, I got this," Dannie said.

TAT! TAT! TAT! TAT! TAT! TAT! TAT!

The shots immediately dropped the beasts, as Dannie hung out the window and continued firing. Kyle honked the horn several times to get the women's attention. They saw the rear passenger door of the Jeep open and immediately headed towards it.

"Get in. Get in," Candice yelled while reaching her arm out the door.

Just as the women begin entering the Jeep, an army of beasts came from the area of the courtyard and began giving chase. Some of them were covered in the orange smoke. Kyle stood no chance advancing towards the beasts, so he slammed the Jeep in reverse.

TAT! TAT! TAT! TAT! TAT! TAT! TAT!

Dannie continued firing from the window, but he knew he didn't have enough bullets to even make a dent in their numbers. "We have to get out of here right now," one of the women barked. The rear passenger door was slammed shut, and Kyle reversed up the curb, allowing Dannie a clear aim at his targets. Spent AK rounds bounced off the passenger side of the Jeep as Dannie fired shot after shot at the beasts. It seemed as if three more emerged every time one went down. When his rifle locked back, Kyle grabbed him by the shirt and pulled him in the Jeep. Kyle sped off in the opposite direction from which they originally came.

"Cover your ears," one of the women yelled.

"What?" Candice asked.

BOOM!

CHAPTER 24

The troops ran for cover as the explosions continued. They were under enemy fire and had to retreat. Tossing grenades towards the insurgents brought them enough time to take cover and return fire. The rattle from the automatic rifle mimicked a typewriter as round after round was being fired towards a row of buildings that were approximately seven hundred feet away from their current location. A large explosion rocked the building, as troops posted in windows and others made their way to the rooftop.

"It's going to be the northwest house of blue three. I copy, over."

"Captain Quinn, I'm running low on ammo," one of the troops yelled, trying his best to be heard over the gunfire.

"Huh?"

"I'm low on ammo," he repeated, pointing to the empty magazines that were dropped by his knee.

"Just hold them off with whatever you have left. Air Support is on their way."

The troops fired into the distance, trying their best to hit their targets. The rounds ricocheting off the brick building established the task was unaccomplished. The enemy continued firing on the troops. Unable to determine their exact location, the troops reloaded and continued the blind assault. Puddles of sweat formed under the shooters as they tried to maintain cover. Giving up their exact location would be a fatal mistake, and their enemies were waiting for the opportunity to kill on behalf of their country. A mixture of gunpowder and brick residue filled the air and subsequently the lungs of the troops that were panting heavily, inhaling as much air as they could. The only thoughts crossing most of their minds were their families back home. That was more than enough motivation to push them to stay alive.

"Captain I'm out. I'm out of ammo," one of the troops complained. Captain Quinn removed an extra magazine from his battle belt, tossing it to the young man who began panicking out of fear. The roar of an approaching aircraft forced everyone to look up. The sight of the McDonnell Douglas F-15E Strike Eagle soaring through the sky gave the troops an extra boost of confidence. They continued firing, demanding the attention of their adversaries while the F-15E prepared for an air-to-ground strike. Gunfire was no longer being fired at the ground troops but was now aimed at the clouds as enemy forces targeted the approaching aircraft. GBU-28s dropped from the sky and onto the intended targets. The explosions shook the earth and turned the row of buildings into a massive pile of rubble. Cheers erupted from the rooftop as the troops watched the debris crumble to the ground. Without the airstrike, there is no telling what would have happened to the soldiers. The position they were in was not ideal, especially with the shortage of ammunition. Although everyone was cheering, Captain Quinn's head was still on a swivel; he didn't underestimate anyone or any situation. He knew the moment they let their guard down and got comfortable; they would become vulnerable. With a wife and daughter depending on him to return home, he stayed focus rather than joining in the celebration.

"Bravo Team, let's move," he ordered, jumping in the stack as his team worked their way back into the building and down the staircase. The troops moved swiftly down each step but halted when they came across a grave discovery. "Why are we stopped?" Captain Quinn asked, pushing through the tight formation. His heart skipped a beat once he finally got to the front of the stack. Seeing as though each troop on the roof was accounted for, the assumption was made that the soldiers that were posted in the windows were inside celebrating their small victory. No distress calls were relayed over the radio, so he had no reason to believe otherwise. That was until they came across the body, sprawled out on the steps. It was the body of one of his troops. A gaping hole in the soldier's face exposed where the enemy fire had hit him. Warm liquid began to fill Captain Quinn's eyes, and he tried his best not to let them fall from his face. He wanted to stay strong at that moment. Strong for the man he just lost and the surviving members of his team. His knee struck the ground as he lowered his body, getting closer to the fallen soldier. Despite knowing the soldier was deceased, he still wanted to pay his respects. "God bless you brother." The soft whisper was gentle, intended only for the person he kneeled before, but the words echoed off the crumbling brick walls. Shaking hands was a clear sign of nervousness, which was the case for Captain Quinn. Reaching around the soldier's neck to remove his dog tags seemed like an impossible feat. Blood soaked through the tactical gloves, causing the chain to slip through his fingers. The dripping gloves went flying across the room, after being ripped off. His hands continued shaking, but they didn't prevent him from performing the task he had done many times before. Separating the clasp made it easy to slide it from around the neck. With the focus on the actions of Captain Quinn, the troops never noticed someone was watching them through the window. They were exposed and didn't even realize the vulnerable position they put themselves in.

BOOM!

CHAPTER 25

"**What the hell was that?**" Candice asked, still rattled from the massive explosion. Glass from the shattered rear windshield dangled from her hair.

"That was a good amount of C-4," one of the women answered. Each occupant in the Jeep was trying to piece together the events that just took place. It was the first time any of them had encountered such a large number of creatures. Although it appeared the colossal blast took care of the beasts, some questions still needed to be answered.

"Seeing as though you too got your grand entrance out the way, do you mind telling us who you are?" Kyle asked.

"Well, I am Cierra, and this is one of my partners, Amanda."

"What were you doing in that courtyard?"

Amanda looked over at Cierra, wondering if they were at liberty to tell the strange group about their mission. Although their discrete display of concern went unnoticed by the rest of the group, Kyle noticed it right away. He slammed on the brakes, causing the rear passengers to jerk forward. He turned and looked back at the women. First, they noticed the grimacing expression on his face and then the small handgun he had pointed in their direction. Cierra repositioned her body and attempted to lean out of the path of the gun, which was pointless because before she knew it Dannie's rifle was up and ready to be used.

"Don't make me have to ask again. What the fuck were you doing in the courtyard?"

"We are researchers. We belong to a group called The Association—"

Kyle's gun was now pressed against Cierra's forehead. Any more pressure on the trigger and her brains would be blown out the back of the Jeep. "Get your fuckin' hands up," Kyle ordered; remembering the boy they left back at the house referenced The Association. The women raised their hands in the air and before they knew what was going on, they felt hands fondling their bodies. Candice wasted no time patting the strangers down and confiscating their weapons. "We know all about your little group and all the pain you cause."

"Pain? What do you mean?"

"Don't play dumb buttercup," Dannie interjected. "You guys do nothing but go around killing helpless people. You are bullies."

"Oh no, you have it all wrong. The Association doesn't kill anyone; we help people."

"So what are these for?" Candice asked, showing the women the guns that were taken from them.

"Protection," Amanda blurted. "We have those to protect us while we are on our research missions."

Candice sucked her teeth. "This is ridiculous, we — we have seen it with our own eyes. Members of your association have slaughtered people. Innocent people." She watched the words that came out her mouth, not knowing what type of response they would receive if they disclosed they were almost victims of The Association's brutal attacks. That tad bit of information would raise suspicions, and it wouldn't be long before someone would realize the group was responsible for the deaths of several members of The Association.

"I don't know where these crazy allegations are coming from, but I promise you we are a friendly group. We take stragglers in and allow them into our community to rebuild what we all have lost. All we want to do is restore our city. Let us take you there," Amanda insisted.

"Hell no," Dannie blurted out. "We ain't going nowhere with yall."

"Ok wait just a minute," Kyle said, thinking about the resources and supplies The Association was probably in possession of. The group was running on fumes and needed a safe place to stay for a while. "Do they have water and food?"

"Yes and plenty of it. We catch rainwater, and we scavenge for food. The Association sends out small groups, and they search for food. You guys would be a great fit for us. Especially with all those moves you just showed off."

"Oh yeah, what exactly were you doing out there?"

"We were investigating a lead we received about a possible habitat for those creatures. One of our groups stumbled upon it a while ago, and we were sent to conduct research. There were supposed to be around ten creatures that linger around, and we were going to study them. That's when hundreds of them suddenly surrounded us."

"And we lost two members of our research team. One of them I'm sure you saw with your own eyes," Cierra added.

The new information hit Kyle and the others like a MAC truck. They all looked around at each other because they could hear the honesty in the women's' testimonies. *They have to be telling the truth. If they are then why were members of the organization slaughtering people?* Kyle was so confused about the organization he had grown to hate in such a short period of time. He still remembered the face of the women who orchestrated the attack on his home, which ultimately led to the death of his wife and daughter. Her dark skin, the large afro, the broken sunglasses, and the disregard for innocent lives. He remembered her all too well. The pain inside his heart still burned and Kyle still wanted revenge. The last thing he wanted to do was jump to conclusions, seeing as though he actually watched the hefty man be ripped to shreds moments before the explosion. Despite witnessing the gruesome attack, he wasn't done with Amanda and

Cierra. "Well, we still need to know what the hell happened out there. What type of research was it? What was up with all that orange smoke? And where the hell did you get those explosives?"

The women looked at each other once more, and Amanda let out a deep sigh. Between their near death experience with the beasts and now having guns pointed at them during an interrogation, they were ready to break down. Tears began to trickle down their eyes as they began to ponder about the details that led up to the explosion. Amanda let out a loud sob as the waterworks began. Cierra wrapped her arm around Amanda and pulled her partner in close. "One of the members of our team that didn't make it was Amanda's brother. He's the one that set off the explosives." The expressions on everyone's faces quickly changed and sympathy worked its way into their hearts. "We were sent out to monitor the area and the creatures because something was attracting so many of them to that specific area for some reason. Once they all popped up Amanda's brother got hurt and couldn't move his leg. He told us to run because he was going to blow the place. The large smoke you saw came from gas canisters he released to attract the beasts towards him, in the center of the courtyard. That orange gas usually attracts the beasts, but once they saw us running, they came after us. The explosion was to ensure none of those things made it out alive. We need to take our land back."

"So what do you think attracted so many of them to that spot?" Candice asked. She rested her hand on

Amanda's leg. Seeing as though she was on the verge of losing her boyfriend once before, she couldn't imagine the pain Amanda felt.

"We aren't completely sure because we didn't have much time at the site before the ambush. I'm sure The Association will send out another team to research whatever is left back there."

"Ok, you've given us the answers we wanted," Kyle said. He did not feel the need to continue the interrogation after listening to every detail about the mission seeing as though Amanda would be reliving the moments of her brother's death. "Where would you like us to drop you off?"

"Drop us off?"

"Yeah."

"Well, our van was probably destroyed in the blast, and we need to get back to The Association."

"I don't think we'll be able to do that."

"Why not? It's too far to walk, especially with these beasts roaming around. Come with us."

"No, we can't do that."

"I'm telling you its ok. They will accept you with open arms."

"I don't think so."

"Trust me; they will. Where else are you going to go? We have food, shelter, security, doctors, teachers, and much more. You don't have to sleep on the streets anymore; you can become one of us."

Kyle cut his eye at Dannie, who had his gun lowered, and then looked at Candice and Marcus. He no longer wanted to be responsible for the group.

Anything that happened to them would be more weight on his shoulders. Jacqui lived to help people, and he thought by dragging them along, he would be fulfilling out her purpose. Kyle had nothing to provide the group, in terms of resources. He had only knowledge, instincts, and survival tactics. Although Candice and Marcus picked up some of his habits, it was time to separate himself from the group. The Association would be able to provide them with everything they needed to survive. They wouldn't have to look over their shoulders at night any longer. Deep down inside, he knew they would or wouldn't approve of his decision, but it was best for him at the moment. He didn't completely trust The Association and couldn't form an alliance with the organization that has caused him so much pain. To avoid a confrontation with the group, he planned to dip out and leave them after they were settled in their new home. "Ok, we are headed to The Association," Kyle announced.

CHAPTER 26

"AGh," Benny Shouted as blood poured from the deep wounds on his left arm. He felt the force from the beast's swipe during their encounter but never realized the claws had dug into his skin. Rob raced through the abandoned cars that filled the streets as he worked his way back to The Association. Once there, The Association would have their medical staff at the camp tend to Benny's injury. The speedometer was right at a hundred miles an hour, as Benny's excruciating screams made Rob floor the gas pedal, in an attempt to save his friend's life. Benny's vision began to blur as he began to dip in and out of consciousness.

"Hold on Buddy; we're almost there." Those words of encouragement fell on deaf ears, and Rob didn't receive a response. He glanced back to see Benny's eyes rolling to the back of his head. Two swift smacks to the face brought Benny back to consciousness, and he began coughing. "Come on man, you better not die on me." Benny didn't mutter a word, but his grunts and groans were enough for Rob to feel confident about his chances of survival.

The Mercury came to a screeching halt as they reached The Association's territory. Rob had to drive slowly knowing that approaching at a high rate of speed would be the perfect reason for the exterior guards to open fire on the vehicle. Rob honked the horn four times, activated the windshield wipers, and flickered his lights, a code that only certain members of The Association were privy to know. The front gate slid open, and he pulled right in.

"You dare return here without my guns or creatures," Micah yelled as he approached the vehicle alongside a crew of ten men.

"I can explain," Rob replied, exiting the Mercury with his hands raised in the air.

"Start explaining!" Micah pressed a shotgun against Rob's chest.

"It was Dale. Dale turned on us. We found the guns and the creatures, but Dale took everything. He tried to kill us, but we fought him off. Benny got injured. He's in real bad shape."

Creases spread across Micah's forehead as he heard the bad news. He glanced past Rob, once he heard the faint groans coming from the sedan. Micah saw Benny and his bloodstained shirt. "Get him out of there and over to the nurses," Micah ordered. Rob quickly turned and with the assistance of three other men, lifted Benny from the vehicle and carried him over to a triage area, a few feet from the customized medical building. Although it was hard for Benny to say a word, he never took his eyes off Rob. He would have never agreed to lie on Dale and basically sign his friend's death certificate. There was no way Micah wasn't going to send a crew to go after Dale, especially if he knew that Dale was tucked away in that small room. Rob avoided all eye contact with Benny as they hoisted his bloody body onto a gurney.

"I want to know exactly where he is," Micah stated as he walked up on Rob. His blood was boiling, and he was tired of Dale's games. Seeing Benny's mangled arm made things worse.

"I can take you right to him sir," Rob replied.

"I'm going to give you a team and want you to bring him back to me, alive. I want to have the honor of slicing that traitor's throat myself."

"Yes, sir."

Micah walked towards headquarters, to begin reviewing which of his soldiers would be joining Rob on the task. A small cramp formed in Rob's torso. The thought of what he just did to Dale was beginning to eat away at his conscious. Dale was nothing but loyal to Rob since they met on their journey to find a safe haven. Wandering the crime-filled streets of Philadelphia, Rob had become a victim of a robbery when three men approached him and took all his belongings. Before the men could turn to run, Dale showed up and demanded they give the items back while he held them at gunpoint. Ironically, the men dropped the items, and Dale still killed them. "It's because of people like that. They're the reason we have to live like this now." He remembered Dale's words so clearly.

Rob walked towards the Mercury but stopped in his tracks when he saw a red Jeep being parked in the designated vehicle lot. It was the same Jeep they took on the mission that ultimately cost them the lives of seven crew members. The fresh bullet holes on the passenger side confirmed his suspicions. A husky male exited the vehicle. He didn't look familiar to Rob, but seeing as though Micah welcomed strangers with open arms; it wasn't unusual to spot an unfamiliar face inside their territory. The male's intuition must have told him something wasn't right because he immediately locked eyes with Rob. The two men shared menacing stares, as Rob's fists began clenching. He wanted to confront the man but knew it wouldn't end well. There had to be a way for him to warn The Association about the new face, without disclosing the error in their ways under Dale's leadership. *I will handle that dude one day when he least expects it.* He watched as the man disappeared behind a building and continued his tasks, while he thought of a new plan.

Rob grabbed the backpack from the backseat. It was soaked in Benny's blood, so he threw it on the trunk of the vehicle, before opening it. *I wonder if there is anything good inside.* His eyes lit up as he began to inventory the bag. The first item he grabbed from the main section of the backpack was a bottle of Vodka that appeared only to be half-full. A box of forty-caliber ammunition and a loaded magazine were also in the bag. Rob turned the bag over and dumped out the remaining items. The contents included a marker, pack of Newport cigarettes, a lighter, a folded up sheet of paper, a pack of gum, and a small cylinder device. Rob licked his crusty lips and wrapped them around one of the cigarettes. The small flame coming from the lighter danced around the tip of the cigarette. He inhaled and filled his lungs with the calming smoke, before releasing it into the air. His hands shook as he handled the cylinder, attempting to open it and reveal its contents. After failing to open the device, Rob discarded it and moved on to check the other items. He slowly unfolded the sheet of paper, while blowing more smoke into the air. Rob's eyes perused the paper, and the cigarette fell from his mouth.

"Micah. Micah," Rob yelled as he searched for the leader. Tripping up the steps, he made his way into the large stone building. "Micah."

"What's going on?" Dre asked after hearing all the shouting Rob was doing. Dre was Micah's younger brother and controlled all aspects of The Association's defense systems and procedures.

"I have to show this to Micah." Rob pressed the paper against Dre's chest. He looked down at it and immediately went to show his brother.

Dre opened the large doors to the meeting room, interrupting Micah and Adina who were lip locking near the window. They both grabbed their guns when the doors swung open. "Sorry to interrupt bro, but you have to see this." Dre slid the sheet across the table, and Adina hovered over Micah's shoulder as he carefully examined the sheet. It wasn't just a sheet of paper; it was a map. He pounded his fist on the paper, rattling the wooden table he was leaning on.

"Where the fuck did this come from?" Micah asked.

"Rob found it," Dre responded, turning around and signaling for him to enter the room.

"Where did you find this map?"

"When Benny and I were leaving, some guy was getting mauled by one of those beasts. This is his bag, and it was near the car, so Benny grabbed it. I started going through the bag, and once I realized what it was, I brought it right up."

"What else was in the bag?"

"Some ammo, cigs and some metal can that I can't get open."

Micah turned to Adina who was holding the map in her hand. They always planned for this to happen, but didn't think it would be this soon. "Our whole area is circled on here."

"Yeah, somebody definitely planned to get here. We have to find out who they are and what they want."

"What do you think they want, baby? We know what they want. They want our empire. We have food, shelter, guns, and numbers. That's what they want, all of it."

"Wait, let's not get ahead of ourselves. Rob said it was only one guy. What if he was coming for refuge? What if he just wanted to join us?"

"Are you sure he was by himself?" Adina asked Rob.

"I — I honestly don't know. There was no one else around. I assume if he was traveling with a group, that they would have helped him. He was literally being eaten alive by one of those monsters, and no one was around to help him."

"See that's exactly what I'm talking about. Nobody is going to let something happen to one of their own without putting up a fight. Plus, he had the map. They wouldn't just abandon the guy that has the directions to where they want to go. That doesn't make sense," Micah stated.

"Well, how did he know we were here? Our entire area is circled, which means he had to be close enough to our territory to mark it down. If he was that close, why wouldn't he just come up to us?"

"Who knows Dina. I just don't want to overreact and make this out to be something it isn't."

"And I don't want to be unprepared if someone plans to take what we have."

"Listen, I will bump up the guards and get our search teams prepared for any encounters we may run across. They did a great job out there earlier and brought us back some new bodies, and one of them is close to you. There are probably thousands of more people out there that deserve a chance at a new life. Life beyond ruin and devastation. The more we grow, the more powerful we will be."

"We need to rule with an iron fist. Fear is true power. This country was built on bloodshed, and we will rebuild it in the same manner."

"That bloodshed will make us targets, and one day we will have to answer for our sins. Are you ready for that?"

"Are you?"

"I'm willing to die for my beliefs and The Association's cause."

"Me too."

It was something about Micah's leadership that drove Adina crazy. Who would have thought a woman that bounced around from shelter to shelter and an ex-convict would have built such a strong organization. "Can you guys leave," she requested as Dre and Rob exited the room and closed the door behind them. Micah laughed, knowing the little heated exchange they had was driving Adina wild. Everything about Micah was intoxicating to Adina. The way he protected her and their people warmed her heart. She placed the map on the table and wrapped her arms around his neck. Micah's hands rested on her hips as he gazed into her deep brown eyes. He pulled her body into his, ensuring they felt each other. Adina's grip around Micah's neck tightened as she began feeling a tingling sensation in her stomach. Their lips touched, and both of their bodies began to warm up. "Promise me you will protect our kingdom," she asked, just before leaning in for another kiss. Her soft lips would have convinced Micah to go to war with the entire world, so Adina's small request was easy to follow up on.

"I promise."

CHAPTER 27

Raw, bedeviling misery filled the atmosphere. Darkness surrounded Dale. He was suffocating on pain and vengeance. The world seemed to be crumbling around him, and there was no one around to help pick up the pieces. It had been hours since he returned to the home with Benny and Rob, but they were long gone. They didn't know what to say to the broken man that sat in the shadows, next to the remains of the woman he loved and the beast that snatched her soul away from him. Two strong reminders that he had nothing else to live for in the new world.

Dale's trigger finger was itching as he held the pistol to the side of his head. Without Dana, he was empty and alone. He was haunted by the souls of the dead; the souls he snatched the lives from. It had been months since he was able to close his eyes in peace, without having to worry about nightmares. The faces of his victims always appeared in his sleep, and the guilt of taking their lives was a heavy burden he carried around daily. *I don't deserve to be here*, he thought. The pressure from his grip removed the slack from the trigger. The shot would ease the pain from all of Dale's sins, and he would finally be at peace. He would no longer be around to cause havoc and hurt anyone.

Just as Dale was about to put himself out of misery, a faint light flashed from under the bed. *What the fuck is that*? He was ready to pull the trigger, but curiosity got the best of him. In a world where necessities such as electricity and running water had become a thing of the past, he had to know what was generating the light and how was it operable. Dale crawled toward the light, which had dimmed. He reached out and grabbed the source of the light. It was an Apple iPhone, and a low battery message displayed on the home screen. *Dana probably dropped her phone*, he thought as he held the device up. He remembered how she always took selfies when they spent time together. The last thing he needed was to see her face because of the circumstances, but he knew looking at her pictures would give him some form of closure. Pressing the circular home button with his thumb, access was gained into the device. The camera app was already open, which allowed Dale to thumb through the saved photos.

Anger washed over Dale, blanketing all else as he looked at Dana's photos. Moments prior, Dale wanted to run from his sins, but seeing the photos was a grim reminder as to why he had to sin. Dana's photos weren't cute selfies, raunchy flicks or memories from her life before the epidemic. Dale scrolling back and forth between ten photos taken of her while she was tied to the bed. They were clearly taken before she was mauled to death and two more photos were taken after the horrific event. Dale had stumbled upon a video that appeared to be recorded from inside a vehicle, which showed him and his crew capturing the very beast he shot in the head. The same beast that made a meal of Dana.

Dale paused, speechless. His recollection of that day was fresh, and he couldn't believe someone had gotten close enough to the group to record them. They were supposed to be clearing out all vehicles and buildings, but somehow the person that recorded the video slipped by unnoticed. *I shouldn't have left Dana alone. I wouldn't if I knew someone was lurking around and watching us.* There was no chance in hell Dale would have let the stranger live if they would have spotted him. That fact was eating him alive because he knew that moment could have saved Dana's life. Dale's head was as clouded as the polluted air around him. His face was glued to the phone as he began skimming through more photos and videos. Disbelief throbbed in his head, and he hoped that at any minute he would awaken from the brutal nightmare. Dale never experienced that type of pain before, so it had to be unreal.

Dale studied the face that filled eighty-five percent of the photo album. He was looking directly at the person responsible for Dana's death. A sick individual that found her demise entertaining enough to record on his phone, along with many others. There had to be close to thirty bodies that were notches on the belt of the young, ostentatious man in the pictures. Dale had never encountered anyone that was as ruthless as he was, but it seems he would soon meet his match. His determination and urge to kill would not be satisfied until he ripped the man's heart from his chest. A new type of evil was emerging from the middle-aged murderer, and it planned to take no prisoners in this war. The Reaper was born.

CHAPTER 28

AFTER PARKING THE JEEP, Marcus walked caught up to the rest of the group who were receiving a short tour of the territory. He looked back to see if he was being followed by the weird man that was eyeing him up. Marcus knew something wasn't right about the exchange, but he couldn't quite put his finger on it. His initial thought was that the older white male that was eyeing him up could possibly be racist and didn't approve of seeing a young black in his territory. That was an issue he faced his entire life, so he wouldn't be surprised if the nasty and hateful habits of the old world had carried over. Whatever the issue was, he knew he had to stay vigilant because there was no telling when he would see the man again.

"Marcus, you made it back, so I'm assuming you found the parking lot with no issues?" Jin asked.

"Yeah, I found it," he replied, still looking over his shoulder.

"Did you leave the keys on the seat as instructed?'

"Yup."

"Good," Jin replied before turning to the group. "The keys are always left in the vehicles because we share everything we have. When we send people out on missions, they have access to weapons and vehicles at will." The small, Asian man reached into his white lab coat and pulled out small bottles of water, handing them to each of the new guests and Cierra. They wasted no time chugging down the lukewarm liquid as it moistened their dry throats. Once they arrived, Jin ordered Amanda to be with the rest of her family to grieve the loss of her brother. He was in charge of overall lab operations for The Association. As a former Chemist, he was interested in studying the mutations as well as the effects the chemical gas had on the earth. Jin was a brilliant man, and he was definitely an asset to the organization. He hoped to find a cure for the mutations and help in rebuilding humanity, but he had a ton of research to do before that could happen.

"Our first stop will be the laboratory, where we conduct small experiments. I must warn you, there are some creatures inside and they are harmless, so you shouldn't be alarmed," Jin advised as he led the group to a large warehouse and swung open the large double doors. The group entered the makeshift laboratory, with its dim lighting courtesy of solar panels that covered the roof of the building. When everyone heard the word *laboratory*, the group expected the sterile all white environment with secure access doors, but this was entirely different. The environment seemed more like a sweatshop than a laboratory. Everyone was dressed normally, besides a few individuals that wore white lab coats like Jin. They seemed to be in charge because they were pacing back and forth while barking orders at groups of people that seemed to be hard at work.

"What are they doing?" Candice asked, noticing everyone in that part of the building had the lower portion of their faces covered with t-shirts, scarves, and masks.

"They are mixing the formula we use to recreate the chemical gas the government created," Jin replied.

"Recreate?"

"Yes, we can't completely duplicate the gas, so we are trying to get as close as possible to the real thing. We are running low on originals, so we have to find a way to imitate it. They are all protecting themselves from breathing in the toxic particles that cause the mutation."

"So where did the originals come from?" Kyle asked wondering how such a powerful weapon got into the hands of street thugs.

"You're going to laugh at the story," Jin stated while chuckling. "Right after Micah claimed this area, he took a crew out to search around, and they came across a military convoy that was passing through town. Micah and the crew needed weapons, so they attacked the convoy. Both sides had a ton of casualties, but Micah was able to secure the vehicles, the weapons, and some of the troops."

"What do you mean some of the troops?"

"During the attack, some of the troops surrendered. Micah isn't an evil man and he let them know he was only after the weapons, to start over fresh. Most of the troops now live here and are in charge of our Defense Operations and overall security for the leaders."

"You said most. What happened to the others?"

Jin's head sunk into his chest and he continued the tour of the facility. As the group walked past the first section of the building, they gave each other weird looks seeing as though the last question about the captured troops went unanswered. Large barriers separated the warehouse. Some doors allowed access to each separate area, and those doors were heavily guarded. Each guard recognized Jin and allowed the group access to the different sections. They entered another large area of the building, where different types of animals were being stored. The smell of feces and wet fur reminded the group of farms and the local zoo. There were several cats, dogs, horses, deer, chickens, monkeys, and even a huge tiger. They were all in cages and had individuals walking around them taking notes on clipboards. No one from the group said a word. There was no question what was going on in the room. Animals have been the subjects of chemical testing for centuries, and it was clear that hadn't changed in the new world. The room was noisy with all the sounds the different animals were making, but there was loud banging coming from the room next door. The guards opened the next door, and Jin continued showing the group the facility. As they entered the next room, a foul smell lingered in the air. It was much worse than the animals but much more familiar to the members of the group. Cages were being rattled, bars were being thumped against, and the sound of fast-paced footsteps set the tone for the room. Kyle couldn't believe his eyes once he saw more than fifty beasts sitting in cages throughout the room.

"You asked about the other troops that didn't comply with The Associations new way of living, well here they are. Micah didn't approve of slaughtering troops that had just surrendered, so he gave them a different type of sacrifice for their country. We tested the gas on them along with others, since it had very little effect on the animals."

Kyle walked past Jin, bumping him with his shoulder. He sent a clear message to the little man in charge of the laboratory that he did not approve of their methods and practices. He walked up to the first cage, staring at the beast that seemed to be full of rage. As Kyle got closer, the beast rammed the cage and attempted to free itself. It would have ripped Kyle to shreds if it were successful. Kyle's hand wrapped around an object that dangled from the cage. He brought it close to his face, while he still kept an eye on the beast. "Sergeant Jonathon Greene, U.S. Army," he muttered as he read the name on the set of dog tags he grabbed.

"Interesting," Jin said as he approached and stood by Kyle's side.

Kyle looked over at the little man in disgust. He wanted to slap the glasses off his flat face.

"It seems like the beast calmed down once you grabbed the dog tags and said his name. We have never seen this happen before. It was as if he remembered his name." Two researchers walked over to the two men and began jotting down notes. "Pass me the dog tags," Jin ordered, sticking his hand out towards Kyle.

"No."

"Listen, young man; you are a guest here. Please hand over the tags."

"I'm not going to repeat myself."

One of the researchers pulled out a handgun and aimed it right at Kyle's head. "Hand it over," the man stated, taking the safety off the gun.

"Don't do it handsome," Dannie said as he aimed the AK-47 at the gunman. Only he knew the gun was empty and it was only a bluff to spare Kyle's life. Dannie used up all his ammunition during the great escape at the courtyard.

It didn't take long for the guards to start pointing guns at the group and Candice and Marcus aiming back at them. It was about to be a bloodbath in the warehouse. "Now everybody just calm down." Jin threw his hands in the air and stood in front of Kyle because he knew nothing good would come of a gun battle in the research facility. "Listen, sir, just hand me the dog tags and no one will get hurt." Kyle extended his arm and tossed the tags at Jin. He watched as the dog tags flew by Jin's head and directly into the cage. "Oh come on. Why did you go and do that?" Jin looked at the tags and knew there was no way they were getting them out from under the three hundred pound creature that once owned them. The beast stepped forward and pressed its face against the cage, before letting out a loud roar. The roar caused everyone's guns to focus on the beast, not knowing what it was capable of doing.

"How the hell did you get involved in this and how do you know so much about those troops?" Marcus asked.

"Because he was in the convoy when it was attacked. Weren't you?" Kyle followed up.

"Yes, yes I was," Jin replied. "I was in the convoy when Micah hit it. I was on the truck with the gas. I used to work for the army and helped conduct research on the gas before the government released it. Since I had knowledge of how the gas worked, Micah spared my life, and I was able to encourage him to spare the lives of the soldiers that wanted to help rebuild America."

"That is fuckin' pathetic. So you are basically responsible for everything that has gone wrong in our country. Including the death of my family." Kyle grabbed Jin by the throat and slammed him against the wall. "Where is the cure for this disease?"

"There isn't one," the choking man mumbled as Kyle's grip tightened and Jin's airway began closing.

"That's enough Kyle, drop him," Candice ordered. She couldn't help but feel bad for Jin as she watched his round face turn red and his movements began to slow down. Kyle dropped the little man to the floor and walked towards the next cage.

"Dr. Lee, are you ok?" Cierra inquired, worried about her mentor who was clearly in pain.

"Yes, I'm fine. He is just a hurt man. He has a chain around his neck, and I'm sure dog tags are hanging from it. Let him be," Jin replied as he began to cough. He stood up and readjusted his tie. He signaled for the guards to stand down. It hadn't been the first time someone's emotions got the best of them, and Jin became the receiver of a brutal attack. Hidden under his lab coat were scars that told intense stories. It wasn't much in the new world that scared the little man. Learning the art of Jiu Jitsu allowed Jin to defend himself against the largest adversaries. He would have given Kyle a run for his money if he wanted to. He watched how Kyle walked towards each cage without fear and saw a form of compassion in his interaction with the beasts. The beasts growled, roared and lunged at him, but not once did he flinch or show any form of aggression back towards them.

"You seem to be gentle with the creatures. Have you been studying them as well?" Jin asked Kyle.

"We came in contact with these things during our journey. They definitely retain the human intellect in the way they search and hunt, but there is also the strong animal instinct that attracts them to each other and to that damn gas."

"Very impressive." A deep voice echoed as it bounced off the walls. "It seems our new guests know these creatures very well."

"Oh, what a pleasant surprise," Jin stated as he turned to see the leaders of The Association standing behind the group. "Everyone, I'd like to introduce you to Micah and —"

"— Dee Dee."

There were only two people in the world that had ever called her by that nickname. Adina looked like she saw a ghost, as she watched the young man run towards her. It had been such a long time since she saw him and since the epidemic, she figured he was dead or rotting away somewhere in a jail cell. She broke out in a full sprint towards him. They looked like a couple prancing through the fields in a typical romance movie. Their embrace was so tight Adina squeezed the life out of Dannie. Tears poured from his eyes as he wrapped his arms around the woman that changed his life. He considered her a sister to him, but she was more of a motherly figure in his life. Once she was arrested for a theft in New Jersey, they lost contact.

"O-M-G sis, I almost didn't recognize you with these braids. You slayin' these boo," Dannie said, referring to Adina's new hairstyle. Dannie was so used to seeing Adina with big, bold hair that rose above her perfect chocolate face. He admired the beautiful, strong woman that stood in front of him and she admired the mature, fearless man that stood in front of her. She eyed him up, and by the outfit he wore, she could tell he had grown to accept who he was.

"Wait, is that...Star?" Adina picked up the small dog and immediately felt the moist, warm tongue run across her cheek. She hugged Star almost as tight as she hugged Dannie. She was the third member of their little family and was always by their side. Adina's face was covered in saliva by the time Star was done with her.

"I'm so proud of you. I missed you so much lil' bro," Adina stated, pulling Dannie in close for another hug. "Where have you been?"

"On the streets, basically. You know I was still hittin' a few licks here and there, but nothin' big. I searched for you, sis. I went to every shelter in the city, but you were just a ghost."

"I got booked out Jersey, and you know how they are out there. They threw the book at me and the rest is history."

"Pinch me."

"Pinch me first." They both couldn't help but laugh, as they finally realized all eyes were on them. Micah extended his hand out to Dannie, who gave it a firm shake. Many nights he listened to Adina talk about the closest person she had to family, and it was an honor to meet the young man finally. He had never seen Adina this happy before and was glad she had another reason in her life to smile. Everyone was all smiles, except Kyle. Seeing Dannie and Adina being reunited made him think of his family. He would kill to experience the feeling of seeing their faces one last time. Kyle couldn't take it any longer and stepped out the warehouse.

CHAPTER
29

The mission seemed as if it would be an easy one. Searching for supplies and survivors was much different that creeping around, trying to avoid everything and everyone. Kyle had grown accustomed to having Candice and Marcus by his side; it felt a bit awkward to be out on the streets without them. They stayed behind with Dannie, to figure out what their assignments will be in the organization. Word got back to Micah about how Kyle snapped on Jin and decided to recruit the man for Adina's search team. Riding around with a group of eight people seemed to be a lot more secure than his original group of three. With eight people, they would be able to cover more ground and their searches would be much quicker. Kyle sat back in the seat and checked out the scenery as the group caravanned in three different vehicles. Kyle rode shotgun in a beat up Ford Explorer, which trailed behind a Chevy Silverado and a Saturn Vue. He was amazed at how much territory The Association was able to claim and clear out. As presentable as the leaders of The Association made their organization seem, Kyle got a bad vibe about them. Something was not sitting right with him, but he couldn't put his finger on it. There were so many questions left unanswered. The Association had no explanation for the innocent lives that were lost at the hands of their men.

After forty-five minutes of driving, the vehicles pulled over onto a deserted block. There wasn't a soul in sight. Kyle carefully scanned each home, and they appeared to be undisturbed. His main focus was on the windows above, which is the vantage point he had when executing intruders. If someone was perched up in the window, his chances of returning fire would be higher than the other shooters he was accompanied by. All of the vehicle doors flung open, and men began exiting. No one left the Chevy, so only Kyle and four others hit the streets. Being the loner he had always been, Kyle began checking the vehicles on the street while the others began checking homes. "Let us know if any of those vehicles have keys in them. We can take them with us," the driver of the Chevy yelled out. Kyle nodded, confirming he acknowledged the order. He peeked in each vehicle, aiming his rifle and ready to fire on any opposition. If anyone dared to pop up from one of the seats, Kyle was ready to put them down. Each vehicle was mostly cluttered with trash and loose change. Three vehicles had the keys inside, and they would serve as nice additions to The Association's growing collection.

"Please stop. Why are you doing this?"

The desperate begging caught Kyle's attention as he peered over his shoulder to see where it was coming from. A middle-aged man was being dragged from one of the homes. Kyle's brows lowered as he saw how roughly the man was being handled. Being dragged by his legs, the man's back scraped across the uneven cement as the coarse ground ripped his skin. For an organization that was all about growing in numbers, they sure weren't treating the fragile man with much respect. *Who would want to join a group that roughs them up?* Kyle thought, remembering how sincere Micah seemed when discussing the organization's expansion plans.

"Who are —"

CRACK!

The man's statement was interrupted by the force of a baseball bat striking the back of his head.

"What the fuck are you doing?" Kyle raised his gun and aimed it at the bat-wielding man. With the slightest movement, Kyle was going to place a bullet between his eyes.

"Calm down dude. You are the new guy right?" one of the other members asked, stepping between Kyle and his target.

Kyle didn't entertain the question, he just looked past the man's slim figure and had his rifle locked on his target's head. "Lower your weapon." The order forced Kyle to eye up the man that felt brazen enough to bark orders at him. He had no idea of what Kyle was capable of doing to him, or the skilled marksmanship that would lay him to rest. On the other hand, Kyle didn't realize he was eyeing up Wolff who was one of the organization's most loyal and dangerous members. The ginger male was hardly intimidated by the former vet's grimacing stare. His left hand had a strong grip on the gun he kept close to his hip, as his right hand combed through his orange beard. A cut off denim vest fit loosely on his shoulders, and his skinny Gap jeans fit snug around his slim waist and rested on top his black Vans sneakers. His strong reputation made up for everything he lacked in stature. His persistence and loyalty had gained him a powerful position directly under the current leaders. Tattoos covered both arms, as the colorful sleeves of ink told a story of his life through precise detail. From the sea of skulls on his forearm to the shredded Irish flag that draped his shoulder blades, Wolff was proud to display his heritage as well as his demons.

"Who the fuck are you talking to?" Kyle asked Wolff, his rifle still aimed at his target.

"Listen, you need to lower your weapon. This isn't your fight," Wolff replied. He was taken back a bit because no one ever disrespected him in that manner and got away with it.

"Our job is to look for resources and bring people back when we come in contact with them."

Wolff laughed at the naïve response. "Who told you that?"

"Micah told me that."

As soon as those words left Kyle's lips, the entire group burst out in laughter. Kyle's eyebrows moved closer together, and the wrinkles on his forehead became more visible, as he looked around at the laughing men. For some odd reason, they became amused once he mentioned Micah's name. This type of disrespect did not sit well with the former soldier. In his opinion, there needed to be a level of respect shown to the ranking members of the organization and clearly, there wasn't.

"We don't answer to Micah," Wolff snarled. "And seeing as though you were chosen to roll with us that means you don't answer to him either."

"Well, who the hell gave us the authority to drag an innocent man from his home and beat him like an animal?" Kyle asked as he stepped forward, getting face to face with Wolff. It looked as if the two men were being showcased at a weigh-in for a pay-per-view boxing match. Despite Kyle's stockier frame, Wolff didn't back down. He turned the trucker hat he was wearing around and got eye to eye with Kyle, showing him that he was ready for whatever move that was about to be made. The other members of the group began circling Kyle. The readjustment of their grips on their weapons showed they all had one intention. Kyle felt their presence surrounding him but kept his eyes fixated on the ginger male standing in front of him.

"BACK DOWN." The direct order caused the group members to back away from their newest member. It also made Wolff take a few steps back from Kyle. Turning his hat back around, he acknowledged the powerful figure that exited the Chevrolet Silverado. A pair of boots clicked on the hot ground, as the sound became louder with each step. Kyle felt a hand touch his shoulder softly and turned to see whom it belonged to. His heart skipped a beat when he saw who had approached. The hand slid from Kyle's shoulder and worked its way down to his hands. Chills fluttered up his spine once he felt the warm palm graze the back of his hand. He felt his rifle being pulled away from his hand. His body was frozen due to the shock he was in. The only movement was Kyle's eyes blinking when the sound of the rifle firing traveled in his ears. He watched as the rifle was raised and a bullet was sent through the skull of the battered man that was lying on the hot ground.

"I know what Micah told you, but things are going to be done my way."

Kyle was shocked to hear those words, especially coming from Adina. Although her words were deceiving, her appearance had his attention. The sun blazed down, bouncing off her chocolate skin. Adina was the definition of perfection when it came to her exterior, but inside she carried around demons from the past and present. Adina had taken her braids out, so her hair stood up straight like it was reaching towards the sky. Her large afro was distinguished and allowed her to tower over average-sized men. The Association's second in command had given orders that contradicted the vision of her counterpart. Her vision was of a world that bowed down to their organization in fear. The neighborhoods they caused havoc in were once homes to hardworking, middle-class residents. The same people that looked down upon those who struggled to live a life that barely crossed the line of poverty. The same people would cross the street when they walked by a shelter, to avoid being in the presence of degenerates like Adina. She felt they were the problem with the country and would not allow them or the rich to survive in the new world unless they proved to be beneficial in the enhancement of The Association. The man that was dragged from the house served no purpose to her, so she did what she has done many times before. The sinister grin that spread across her face displayed her willingness to execute the innocent for her evil cause.

"If you are not with The Association, you are against us," she announced. The members of her small group broke out in loud cheers and praise for their leader. Kyle was still stuck as the demonic cheers drowned out his thoughts. Adina basked at the moment, gliding over to Kyle and handing him back his rifle.

CRACK!

Kyle drove the rifle stock straight into Adina's nose, breaking it. Blood poured from her nostrils as he held her in a chokehold. The barrel of the rifle kissed the back of her head, as Kyle backpedaled away from the rest of the group. The warm fluid dripped down his forearm as he tightened his grip. The broken sunglasses Adina wore were completely shattered when she was struck in the face. There were multiple guns pointed at Kyle, and he kept Adina close to prevent a clear shot. He wasn't too worried about anyone except Wolff, who was focused on him.

"What the fuck are you doing?" Adina asked, choking on her blood.

"Central Avenue," Kyle replied.

"What?"

"Central Avenue." He pressed the rifle harder against her head.

"Agh." Adina cringed in pain as the force from the rifle felt as if it was piercing into her head.

"We can't save everybody. That guy wouldn't have done anything for us, so why avenge his death?"

"His death? I'm not worried about him. You really don't remember?"

"Remember what?"

"Central Avenue. Your men attacked my home, and I lost my family."

"I don't know what you're talking about. What does that have to do with me?"

"They were under your orders. You allowed them to do what these men were doing today. Their blood is on you."

The other members of the group looked around at each other, trying to figure out what the next move was going to be. Kyle was continually backpedaling, while they slowly advanced.

"Back the fuck up, or I will blow her brains out."

"If you do that I will kill you myself and you can go visit your family in hell," Wolff shouted. He was a man who stood behind every decision he makes and his sins did not haunt him. Guilt never crossed his mind. He could care less about Kyle's grief; he wanted blood. He aimed his pistol but did not have a good shot. He was confident to take it but didn't want to risk the safety of his leader. Noticing the loyal ginger was not backing down, Kyle was running out of options. He could attempt a shot at the man, but the passive resistance Adina was displaying was an indicator that she would put forth an effort to escape when she had the opportunity to do so. Squeezing tighter on her neck, the tenseness she was displaying began to fade.

"Throw one of those canisters on your hip," Kyle whispered in Adina's ear. Right before she shot the man on the sidewalk, he noticed two canisters on her hip. Adina didn't immediately respond to Kyle's request and began wiggling around trying to free herself from his strong hold. This caused Kyle to squeeze harder, crushing her trachea. "Throw the canister at them and don't try anything else." The strong leader had no more fight left in her. Struggling to breathe, she gasped for air as blood trickled into her mouth. Her adrenaline wasn't pumping as much, and the pain from her wrecked nose was shooting through her entire face. No one had ever violated her in such a way and for the first time in years, she was afraid. Something about the former soldier rubbed her the wrong way. He was strong; too strong to break. Compliance would be the likely key to her survival. She reached down and grabbed one of the canisters. The members of the group were so focused on Kyle; they never saw the gestures made by Adina. Orange smoke began to seep from the canister, as Adina removed the pin from the device. She tossed the canister towards the group of men.

"Move, move, move," Wolff ordered as they began to scatter, avoiding exposure to the gas. His gun was still aimed towards Kyle during his retreat.

The smoke began to spread throughout the air, as the wind blew the particles around. Kyle had no way of reaching for his mask; if he did, it would mean removing his arm from around Adina's neck. It was time to get out of the area. The smoke covered Wolff's silhouette, and Kyle no longer had a visual on his adversary. A sharp sting shot through Kyle's forearm as he felt a strong clamp pinch his skin. Adina's last attempt at freedom was effective. Her bite broke the skin on the arm of her capturer and loosened his grip from around her neck. The rifle was still pressed against her head, but she attempted to run.

BANG!

...TO BE
CONTINUED

WATCH FOR THE NEXT SCAVENGER NOVEL

THE SCAVENGER HUNT

AVAILABLE FALL 2018

AVAILABLE NOW

COMING SOON...

C.L. LOWRY
THE
GUILTY
VERDICT

C.L. LOWRY
Stray
BULLET

PRETTY
Savage
C.L. LOWRY

THE
INSIDE
JOB
C.L. LOWRY

About the Author

C.L Lowry is a novelist and short-story writer, with no bounds. Along with writing suspenseful novels for mature audiences, he touches on current social issues in America. C.L. Lowry spent over five years in law-enforcement and uses his experience and education to demand his readers' attention with realistic scenarios throughout his stories.

C.L. Lowry was born and raised in Philadelphia, Pennsylvania. In June of 2016, his debut novel The Black Badge: Confessions of Corruption ranked #4 on Amazon's Top 100 Best Selling Crime Fiction books. The Black Badge: Confessions of Corruption also won an award for the best book under the Anthologies & Compilation's category at the 2016 New York Book Festival.

If you have any questions, suggestions, complaints or want to volunteer as a beta reader and receive free advance-reading copies of new books, please email C.L. Lowry at CreedomPublishing@outlook.com. For more information on C.L. Lowry and book release dates visit www.creedompublishing.com.

Creedom Publishing Company

Creedom Publishing is a fully incorporated publishing company. Much like our slogan "The Home of Creative Freedom," we are committed to providing new and upcoming authors with the resources and opportunity to share their *creativity* with the world. At Creedom Publishing, writers have the *freedom* to make their own choices, without the burden of committing to one-sided contracts and guidelines that most traditional publishing companies offer. We are located in the Philadelphia area of Pennsylvania. Creedom Publishing also provides services for nonprofit organizations, such as CrimeFighters Inc. and much more.

Our books are available for purchase on our site and eBooks are available through Amazon Kindle.

CONTACT THE CREEDOM PUBLISHING COMPANY AT:

CREEDOMPUBLISHING@OUTLOOK.COM

OR BY MAIL AT:

CREEDOM PUBLISHING COMPANY
P.O. BOX 1336
ROSLYN, PA 19001